WILD

More books by Lucy Courtenay

More from Hodder Children's Books

WILD

Bear Hug

LUCY COURTENAY

Hodder
Children's
Books

A division of Hachette Children's Books

Typeset in AGaramond by Avon DataSet Ltd,
Bidford on Avon, Warwickshire

Printed and bound by CPI Group (UK) Ltd, Croydon, CR0 4YY

The paper and board used in this paperback by Hodder Children's Books
are natural recyclable products made from wood grown in
sustainable forests. The manufacturing processes conform to the
environmental regulations of the country of origin.

Hodder Children's Books
a division of Hachette Children's Books
338 Euston Road, London NW1 3BH
An Hachette UK company
www.hachette.co.uk

For my goddaughter Grace.

With special thanks to
Chris Brown of Tooth 'n' Claw
and Dr Debra Bourne MA VetMB PhD MRCVS.

1

Curtain of Awkwardness

Sinbad the Bengal tiger was roaring over his breakfast and making the windows rattle in our kitchen.

The sounds of Wild World, local safari park and – as of the week before Christmas – our new home, hadn't got normal yet. I was pretty sure they never would, which was cool by me. Adopting what I hoped was a casual 'I hear roaring tigers every day' position at the kitchen table, I pored over the local paper in front of me.

'Pass it over, dimbo.'

I looked up. My twin sister, Tori, was beckoning impatiently for the paper.

'I'm still reading our horoscope,' I objected. *Dimbo?* 'Listen. "Prepare for the bright lights as your time in the spotlight has come!" I wonder what it means?'

Tori put on her thinking face. This is exactly like *my* thinking face as we're identical twins, only in Tori's case she really means it. I tend to use it only when I'm trying to look clever in class after a teacher asks me a question. It hides the fact that I'm usually panicking like a wasp trapped in a sticky jam jar.

Tori slapped the table with her hand. 'Got it.'

I leaned forward eagerly in case my sister'd had one of her rare insightful flashes. Dimbo indeed.

'It means,' said Tori, 'that we have a dental appointment this afternoon. And the dentist will shine his little light into your big gob and—'

'Oh, go take a long walk off a short cliff, you geek,' I said. Tori doesn't get horoscopes. *Tele*scopes, yes. *Stetho*scopes, yes. But horoscopes, no.

'Don't tease Taya, Tori *querida*,' said Mum from where she was standing by the sink with a bottle of baby milk in her hand. She sounded weary. 'And, Taya? Don't let your sister annoy you so much.'

If you didn't know about Mum's animal fostering job, you'd be forgiven for thinking just then that she was apparently blessed with a luxuriant beard. A baby chimpanzee clung to her front, holding a grubby brown teddy, his furry head resting against her chin and blending quite nicely with Mum's long brown hair.

Tori tried to pull the paper away from me.

'What do you want it for anyway?' I snarled, grabbing it back.

'I want to read about the film they're making at Harting Park.'

Just in time I stopped my jaw from dropping into my cereal with a clang. Harting Park was only five miles from Fernleigh, our town, and they were making a film there? Like, a proper one with costumes and lights and cameras? Did that mean there were movie stars in the vicinity? Would I bump into someone famous in CostQuik? How come I hadn't heard of it? All these thoughts rushed through my brain like wildebeest aiming for the least crocodile-infested bit of river they can see.

'How do you know about it?' I asked.

Tori shrugged. 'Everyone knows.'

Apart from me, clearly. I tried to look like I was among the 'everyone'. 'Yeah, well,' I said as casually as I could, 'you're not exactly known for having your finger on the pulse of popular culture, are you, Tor?'

'This isn't popular,' Tori said. 'It's *art*. Pavlov Valkyrie's the director!'

'Hmm,' I said vaguely. *Who?*

As Mum took the bottle of milk out of the microwave, Grandpa, the chimp, started making eager little woffling noises, detached himself from her chin and latched on to the teat, dropping his teddy in the process. Rabbit, our ancient golden retriever, gave it a sniff.

'You know,' Tori insisted, raising her voice over the noise of Grandpa's hungry slurping. 'The detail king? Like, everything in his films has to be exactly right or he gets into these famous strops and makes people cry? Come on, Taya, even *you* must have heard of him.'

'Oh, yeah,' I said, none the wiser. 'Pavlov Val . . . what you said. Yup. With you now.'

'Taya, you're *such* an airhead.' Tor pushed her long brown plait over her shoulder and flipped the paper open at the exact right page straight off. The classic front view of Harting Park – all pink brick, and white stone frames around the windows, yellow roses in the flowerbed, and sweeping gravel driveway – loomed out at us in pretty perfection. *Valkyrie to Shoot Period Epic at Harting* went the headline.

Coming round to Tori's side of the table, I barged her away from the article.

'Has it got any animals in it?' I asked. 'There were loads of animals in period times.'

I didn't ask this question because I'm crazy about animals by the way, although I totally am. I asked it because animals on film is our dad's business. The business is called Wild About Animals; our surname's Wild too. Talk about predestined career.

'If you'd let me finish reading it,' Tori said through gritted teeth, 'I might be able to tell you.'

'"Mirza Khan and Polly Richards are named as the main actors in a historical film called *The Ring and The Rose*, shooting at the park over the next month,"' I read, scanning quickly through the rest for any mention of four-legged actors. Nada. Not only was this a major disappointment, but I hadn't heard of the director, the film *or* the so-called stars.

'Sounds a bit serious,' I said when I got to the end. Rabbit lumbered over for some attention and I stroked her big yellow head.

'Serious can be good, you know,' Tori said crossly, rubbing her arm where I'd shoved her.

I rolled my eyes. 'Lighten up will you, you nerd? I was just *saying*—'

'*Enough!*' Mum set down Grandpa's empty bottle on the side, put the baby chimp over her shoulder to burp him and glared at us, sparks shooting from her eyes. 'The sooner you girls go back to school the better. You've done nothing but snip with each other since Christmas.'

This wasn't the time to correct Mum's vocabulary. 'Tori started it!' I said, stung. 'I only snipe at Tori because she snipes at me first! And if I maybe ever sometimes *do* start stuff, it's only to protect myself!'

'But—' Tori began.

'But nothing!' Mum interrupted Tori fiercely. 'Your father—'

She stopped like she'd just run into a Dad-shaped brick wall. Rabbit whined. Silence came down and wrapped us all up in a curtain of awkwardness.

'Dad what?' challenged Tori into the quiet. 'Go on, Mum, say it. What would Dad do? Shall we ask him? Oh no, we can't because you told him to leave in the middle of Christmas lunch last week. That little reconciliation didn't last long, did it?'

I gaped at my sister. Mum went white. Tori looked a bit shocked at what had just come out of her own mouth. Then Grandpa's bottom made a rude and unmistakeable noise. It usually made us laugh, but not today.

'I'll change Grandpa's nappy, Mum,' I said, keen to move the conversation on from this awful place. 'Give him here.'

Mum thrust Grandpa into my arms and stalked wordlessly out of the kitchen. Tori tossed her plait over her shoulder again and stalked wordlessly out of the back door. Rabbit decided Tori's destination was the better option and lumbered after her. Outside, Sinbad roared again.

'Oh well, Grandpa,' I said to the chimp, resting my face against his warm cheek. I scooped up his teddy and let him cuddle it. 'Let's sort out your little stink, shall we? Seeing how we can't do much about the other one around here.'

2

The Whole Pudding Thing

Don't ask me to explain grown-ups.

Before everything went wrong, Mum and Dad were like a pair of embarrassing teenagers at a beach party, all kissy huggy lovey. I hated it when they came to parents' evening at our primary school because it's terrible seeing old people hold hands and, even worse, snog in your classroom. And now suddenly they weren't talking to each other and Dad had moved out and it was all because our house burned down, which seems just too random for words. OK, I guess it was more complicated than that, but what do I know? I'm only eleven.

Anyway, things improved a bit when Mum got the permanent zookeeper-stroke-animal fostering job complete with gorgeous house at Wild World, and Dad had come to see us all on Christmas Day and everything had been fine until the pudding. It burned him in a pretty nasty place when Mum threw it in his lap. Now they just communicated by terse little texts, usually about who was picking us up from where and at what time. Whatever happened to sticking together through the tough times? It looked like our folks had bottled that bit good and proper.

'I'm never getting married,' said Tori as the bus lurched us into town at the end of our first week back at Forrests – school for the Mad, Bad and Wrong Side of Fernleigh kids plus us.

'Who'd marry *you* anyway?' I muttered. We still weren't getting on very well, incidentally, in case you hadn't worked that one out for yourself.

'I would,' Joe Morton piped up. He clutched a little tighter on to his book bag with one knobbly-knuckled hand and gave Tori a bony thumbs-up with the other.

'Cheers,' said Tori gloomily.

'Me and all,' said Cazza Turnbull, Year Seven's Scary Girl Number One and somehow Tori's best mate. She swung round the bus pole at speed, making a couple of non-Forrests people mutter and change seats. 'But I'd so take you to the cleaners when we like, divorced.'

I shuddered at the mention of the D word. No one had said it where Mum and Dad were concerned – at least, not yet.

Tori and I got off the bus in town as we were meeting Dad at the Caramel Café in the town centre. I'd tried to persuade Mum to let Dad come up to Wild World and see us there, but she'd gone on about keeping Grandpa calm and not wanting aggro at her place of work, and most likely remembering the Christmas pudding.

Dad looked grey and miserable, hunched over a cup of tea. His camera was slung round his neck as usual. He's a photographer by training and can't help snapping stuff, wherever he is.

'How's your mum?' was the first question he asked when Tori and I sat down.

'Terrible,' said Tori.

Dad brightened a bit at this. I noticed his little box of sweeteners was lying beside his teacup. That was good, at least. Even with all the Mum traumas, Dad wasn't being daft about his diabetes.

'How was your first week back at school?' was Dad's next question.

Neither Tori nor I particularly wanted to tell him

about the fire in the chemistry lab set by a Year Ten kid who'd been excluded on the first day back, nor the window in the changing rooms that had a stone chucked through it and cut Jonno Nkobe's head, because we knew he'd get narky about the school and we were starting to feel sort of loyal to Forrests. Although it was still pretty much the scariest place ever, we'd got used to it – even maybe liked it a little bit, in the way you sometimes like the ugliest, snarliest guinea pig in the petting zoo, even though it keeps trying to bite your fingers off.

'Fine,' we both said together.

'Any work, Dad?' I asked.

Dad gave a half-smile that was only just visible through his scraggy beard. 'I've got a job on a new film up at Harting Park.'

'I *knew* it,' I said in delight. 'Period stuff always has animals!'

'You're working with *Pavlov Valkyrie*?' Tor asked.

'We read about it in the local paper,' I explained, as Dad was looking surprised that we knew what he was talking about.

'The director on the monkey link we filmed before Christmas recommended me,' he said, stirring his tea. 'And one of Mr Valkyrie's casting assistants, Dave, has asked me to find some circus horses for the film. It's looking straightforward so far.'

I was Officially Excited! OK, so it was a dozy film about the past, where probably nothing happened except card games and a bit of bad dancing, with unknown actors and a director with a silly name – but it was a movie nonetheless and *Dad was involved*!

'I can't believe you're working with Pavlov Valkyrie, Dad,' said Tori. She looked awestruck. 'I mean, *Pavlov Valkyrie.*'

My sister went off into this brainiac daze as I plied Dad with more important questions. 'Is there a part in it for us? What are the costumes like? Why do you need circus horses?'

'The film's based on a real-life incident from the eighteen-nineties,' Dad explained. 'A circus came to a sleepy Berkshire town and the daughter of the lord at the big house eloped with one of the circus horsemen.'

'Oooh!' I said. The film was suddenly sounding better than I'd thought. 'A romance! Is the lead actor really handsome? Are there loads of soppy scenes with everyone wearing fantastic dresses?'

Tori made puking noises quietly into her hand.

'I've got no idea,' Dad confessed. 'I've just been asked to find the horses. I've got an appointment with a circus guy with stables down near Southampton in a couple of weeks' time – do you girls want to come with me? If it's OK with your mum, of course,' he added hastily.

I squealed, making a mental note to twist Mum's arm until she gave in if she had a problem with it. Circus horses! What amazing tricks would they do? Walking on their back legs? Jumping through paper hoops? Riding unicycles? I imagined them: their silky coats rippling with muscles, their heads crowned with great pink plumes, their riders in sparkly sequins to *die* for.

'Don't worry, Dad – she'll be totally fine about it,' Tori promised. Her eyes were gleaming as much as mine. For once, we seemed to be agreeing about something.

'Do you think so? I'll text her the details.' Dad set down his teacup and chewed the side of his thumb. Tori and I do it too, when we're worried. It's clearly a genetic thing. 'How is she, by the way?' he asked. 'Or have I asked you that already?'

'You've asked us already, and she's still terrible,' said Tori.

'Why don't you ring her, Dad?' I said. It was so ragingly clear that he wanted to. 'I think she's regretting

13

the whole pudding thing, you know.'

'She won't answer the phone,' he said. He looked fit to burst into tears. 'I don't know what to do.'

Tor and I both reached for his arm at the same time.

'Don't worry,' I said. 'You'll win Mum back. It's just going to be a question of timing.'

'And avoiding hot items of food,' Tori added.

3

Proper Horse Legs

The weekend passed in a blur of Grandpa stuff. Mum had introduced the little chimp to a comfort blanket instead of his teddy a week earlier, and Grandpa had taken to holding a corner of it in his mouth and sucking it. Now it was time to cut the blanket up and give a piece to Honey, the full-grown female chimp out in the Wild World ape house. Everyone had high hopes that Honey was almost ready to take Grandpa on as his surrogate mum, with some bottle-feeding by the humans along the way. A piece of blanket would give her something with Grandpa's smell on it.

'It seems cruel, keeping Honey and Grandpa apart for much longer,' I said as we sat together in the ape house with Mum and Dr Nikolaides, the Wild World vet, on Grandpa's Sunday afternoon visit. 'Honey is head over heels in love. I mean, *look* at her.'

Honey literally groaned with excitement each time Grandpa was brought to see her. The other chimps weren't especially interested, but Honey's long hairy brown arms stretched out like in those slo-mo romantic moments you see on old films, just before the lovers gallop into each other's arms. Now she sat as close to us as she could, clutching the smelly piece of blanket that Mum had cut off Grandpa's comforter like she was holding Grandpa already, and crooning little chimpy nursery rhymes through the glass. Grandpa fixed his round hazel eyes on her and stared, his own scrap of blanket held tightly against his chest. He was probably thinking: 'Whoa! You're a lot hairier than my mum!'

'I think we can try the handover this week,' said Dr Nik in his gravelly Greek voice. 'What do you think, Anita?'

'Yes, I think they are both almost ready, Jonas,' Mum smiled back at him.

'It's a shame Mum and Dad are married,' Tori remarked vaguely as we headed back through the park for homework and beans on toast. 'I think Dr Nik likes her.'

I was horrified. 'Tori! You can't say that! Mum and Dad *love* each other!'

'I know!' Tori protested, flushing a little. 'I'm just *saying*.'

'Well, *don't*,' I hissed. 'Don't you want Mum and Dad to get back together? So everything can be the same as before?'

Tori's eyes flickered a bit. She dipped her head and stared at the ground. 'Nothing's ever the same as before,' she said.

Our little house beamed cheerfully at us through the late afternoon gloom, the porch light swinging a little in the wind. I gave a little skip as we came through the gate, forgetting for a moment about Tori's dangerous thought directions. We *lived* here. Here, in the wildlife park! Once we sorted out our parental traumas, life had the potential for perfection.

I promised myself there and then to make sure Mum and Dad wouldn't drift apart. They loved each other as much as Honey and Grandpa did, and I wasn't going to see them separated for an instant longer than I had to.

On Monday, Jonno Nkobe returned to school with a bandage round his head as big as a proper turban, so no one got any work done because the boys in our class kept trying to unravel it when Jonno wasn't looking. His mate Tosh nearly succeeded, but was sent to the Head for endangering Jonno's stitches. So we didn't get any work done on Tuesday either because we were talking about Tosh and how he was probably going to get excluded like the arsonist in Year Ten.

'I'm gonna get excluded this term,' Cazza boasted on Wednesday.

'Don't be stupid, Caz,' Tori said. 'Pass us the dictionary.'

Cazza passed Tori the dictionary she wanted. Even though Tori'd been doing this for a couple of months now, I still found it totally amazing how my twin could bring the terrifying Cazza Turnbull to heel like a well-trained dog. Cazza's former best mates, Heather Cashman and Carrie Taylor, looked on enviously. I bet you they never figured out how to get Scary Mary numero uno to do what *they* wanted.

I bit the end of my pen and tried to concentrate on what I was writing. It was hard because English isn't really my best subject, and up to this point in the lesson I'd been devising romantic scenarios in my head where Mum and Dad got back together again, and had not been thinking about work at all.

'Describe a horse to an alien who's never seen a horse before' was the title. *It looks like a big brown animal with ears and a tail and a face that's long like a ruler* was as far as I'd got. I was making the poor creature sound like some kind of freak. Sighing, I glanced around the room for inspiration.

Biro Lohoni had his head down over his book in front of me. For someone who only recently learned to speak English, he's pretty good in English lessons. His handwriting is slow and careful, like his pen is tiptoeing through a minefield. I craned my neck as subtly as I could to see if I could steal a couple of ideas.

A beautifully drawn horse was galloping across the top of Biro's page. He'd got its mane and tail all fluttery, and somehow its legs looked like proper horse legs and not Twiglets. Underneath I could see he was drawing an arrow from the picture to some words underneath that said: *A horse looks like this.*

It took me a couple of seconds to recover from the complete brilliance of a) Biro's drawing and b) Biro's genius example of how to answer the question. Eagerly I began to draw a horse of my own.

'Why have you drawn a dog?' Joe said ten minutes later, peering at my sheet. 'We're supposed be writing about horses.'

'I wish we were doing this in a couple of weeks' time,' I muttered, scrubbing out my dog-horse-thing crossly. 'We're going to see these circus horses with Dad and I would *totally* be able to answer questions about horses then.'

'Aren't circus horses, like, illegal?' asked Cazza from the other side of Tori. Her parents are both lawyers so she sometimes knows about the law.

'Nope,' said Tori. She turned over her sheet and, to my horror, continued writing on the back. 'Horses are usually domesticated, and working in a circus is about the same as showjumping if you think about it. It's not horses we should worry about in circuses, Caz. It's *wild* animals in circuses. The thought of wild animals being snatched from their natural environment and made to do tricks for the fun of humans is totally sickening.'

'That makes your dad's job sickening then,' Heather Cashman said loudly. '*He* makes animals do stuff for the fun of humans.'

Cazza looked surprised, like she'd forgotten her ex-mate could speak. Joe and Biro both shrank away as Tori and I rose from our seats.

'Take that back,' Tori said, flames practically hurtling out of her eyeballs.

Heather slumped back in her chair, pleased to have

got our – or more specifically, Cazza's – attention. 'Tell me the difference between animals on film and animals in circuses and I'll take it back,' she said smugly.

I stopped spluttering and found some words that made sense. 'I . . . It's . . . You don't know *anything* about it! Our dad doesn't *snatch* animals from anywhere and he *never* makes animals do stuff they don't want to do!'

'I bet that's what all the circus owners say,' drawled Carrie Taylor, and Heather guffawed.

'Five minutes!' called Ms Hutson at the front of the classroom as I felt my fingers curl into a fist of destruction. Those two were *so*—

'Don't get busted on Cash 'n' Carrie's behalf, Taya,' Tori sighed. As usual, she had herself back under control way before me. 'They're just annoyed that Caz ignores them these days. *We* know Dad doesn't exploit our animals, and that's what matters.'

I sat down and picked up my pen with so much force I practically snapped it in half. Cash 'n' Carrie kept right on sniggering, in spite of Cazza's best laser stare.

'Horses,' Tori prompted soothingly.

I stared at my page, trying to remember where I'd got to. Horses do have long, flat faces – but somehow a ruler wasn't quite the comparison I was trying to achieve. A tabletop? A wooden spoon? If these aliens had never seen a horse before, the chances of them seeing a wooden spoon were also pretty slim.

In desperation I crossed out everything I'd written and scrawled across the bottom of my page:

A horse looks like what Biro's drawn.

It would have to do.

4

Chimpy Love-In

Joe came over on Thursday afternoon. He'd been desperate to come round to the new house at Wild World since before Christmas, so here we were. You never saw anyone so thrilled in your life.

'I can't believe you live here!' Joe kept saying in a daze, hefting his book bag over his shoulder as we followed Mum, Grandpa and Dr Nik out of the garden gate. 'But I think maybe it was always meant to be this way because you're called Wild and this is Wild World so it's basically your world, isn't it? I mean, can *you* believe you live here? You are so *unbelievably* lucky.'

'We know, Joe,' said Tori patiently.

'*Unbelievable*,' Joe said again.

Mum and Dr Nik had been preparing Honey and Grandpa for the Big Handover all week – and we were about to make Joe's life even *more* complete as we were all going to watch it happen for real.

Grandpa started chattering and reaching out his arms as soon as we set foot in the ape house. As Mum and Grandpa went through to the little en suite-type room at the side of the main enclosure, Honey came galloping over like a rocket had been strapped to her back, the shredded remains of the blanket piece clutched in her hand.

Mum kissed Grandpa on the head and laid him down on the ground. Then she joined us again, shutting the door behind her. From the outside, Dr Nik opened a little door called a 'creep', just big enough for Honey to come through from the enclosure to the en suite.

The next bit happened so quickly that I almost missed it. Honey rushed through the creep, snatched up Grandpa and sprinted back into the enclosure again, making hysterical giggling noises. *Got him! Nah nah, na nah nah!*

'Is he supposed to be upside down?' Joe asked.

Grandpa squealed at the undignified way Honey was holding him. The two male chimps looked over in an interested kind of way as the youngster dug his little paws into Honey's hairy chest and turned himself the right way round.

'That is the most adorably cute thing I've ever seen,' I sobbed, wiping my eyes with the sleeve of my school jumper as Honey and Grandpa had their first proper cuddle.

Mum and Dr Nik looked pretty teary too. As for Joe, I thought he was about to dash into the en suite, squeeze through the creep into the enclosure and join in the cuddle himself.

'Perfect,' Tori said, which was the closest thing to a dramatic display of emotion we were likely to get. Funny how different twins can be, isn't it?

The ape-house door clanged open, making us all jump. Mum and Dr Nik's boss – Matt, the Wild World manager – came hurrying in. His face was even redder than usual and he was out of breath.

'Did I miss it?' he panted.

'Sorry, Matt,' Mum apologized.

Pressing his hand to his side, Matt gazed at the chimpy love-in on the other side of the glass. Honey and Grandpa were nose to nose now. 'Never mind,' he gasped. 'The main thing is . . . it seems to have worked and they're . . . both happy. You'll still be . . .

bottle-feeding Grandpa for a while, I take it, Anita?'

Mum nodded.

'What happened to you, Matt?' Tori asked curiously.

'You look like you've just run a marathon, boss,' said Dr Nik.

Matt wiped his sweaty forehead with the back of his hand. 'The electric buggy broke down after lunch; it's going to take at least a fortnight to fix. I've had to . . . resort to my old bike to get around. There are more . . . hills in this place than I ever realized.'

I looked at the floor as I tried to suppress a giggle. The idea of Matt and his big tummy wobbling around Wild World on a bike was pretty hilarious. I heard a snort from Tori which told me she found the idea just as funny as I did. Joe was still gazing mistily at Grandpa and Honey and didn't react at all.

'Excellent news,' said Mum. 'You don't get enough exercise, Matt. It will be very good for you.'

'Can we expect to see you in the Tour de France next year, boss?' Dr Nik asked.

Tori and I both lost it, which set Mum off. Dr Nik wasn't far behind.

'What's so funny?' said Joe, tearing his eyes from Honey and Grandpa.

Poor Matt was still trying to get his breath back, so

he contented himself with a mock-shake of a fist and a rueful smile. 'I'm glad I caught you anyway, Jonas,' he said to Dr Nik when everyone had recovered. 'I wanted to remind you that our bear's out of quarantine and will be with us tomorrow.'

'It's in the diary, boss,' said Dr Nik with a nod.

Tori and I glanced at each other. What bear?

'What bear?' asked Joe on cue.

'A female brown bear from a Russian circus that went bang in the summer,' Mum explained.

'Went *bust*, Mum,' I said. Mum's Portuguese, so her English gets a bit random sometimes. Exploding bears was a good one.

Mum waved a hand in the air to say, *You know what I meant*. 'She would not survive back in the wild, so Matt agreed to take her here.'

Knowing Mum as I did, Matt probably hadn't had much choice in the matter. When Mum first started in zoology, she'd camped outside the previous Wild World boss's office until he agreed to give her a job. Mum would sail over Niagara Falls in a leaking welly if it meant helping an animal in distress.

'Thanks to your mother, we're developing the rescue side of our conservation work at Wild World very nicely,' Matt said with a wry smile. 'She's taken this one on as her personal project.'

'Was the bear badly treated in the circus?' Tori asked.

I shot her a glance. I knew we were both thinking of Cash 'n' Carrie, and the rights and wrongs of performing animals.

'Possibly,' Dr Nik admitted. 'Apparently she's been very bad-tempered for much of her time in quarantine, which could be a sign of trauma.'

Wild World didn't have any other bears. 'Won't she get lonely all by herself?' I asked, feeling a bit choked.

'Bears are generally solitary animals,' said Dr Nik. 'But she isn't alone.' He smiled before adding: 'She gave birth to three cubs four weeks ago.'

'Cubs!' I squealed, feeling better at once. Adorable!

'But four weeks ago, it was December,' Tori said with a frown. 'I thought bears slept in the winter, not had babies.'

Then Mum said the craziest thing.

'If it is cold enough for hibernation – and we've had a very cold winter this year – they have their cubs while they're sleeping.'

'No *way*!' I gasped. Joe and Tori looked stunned too.

Dr Nik laughed at the expressions on our faces. 'It sounds impossible, but it's true.'

I didn't know what to make of that. Imagine going to sleep and then waking up to find three cubs staring at you!

'Adult bears drift in and out of sleep in the cold weather, depending on what's going on,' Dr Nik explained. 'The quarantine unit fed her well in the summer and kept the temperature low in her quarters, so she has been sleeping deeply. Cubs don't need much in the early days – just peace, darkness and milk. And the mother doesn't need to be wide awake to give them her milk, does she?'

'Brown bears were once native to the UK,' Matt added. 'Did you know that?'

How much more astonishment could I take in five minutes? 'Bears in this country? Like, wild bears?'

'No, Taya, you doughnut,' said Tori. 'Bears on little collars and leads.'

'Imagine meeting a bear on Fernleigh Common like you sometimes meet foxes,' said Joe in awe as I tried to give Tori a Chinese burn.

'They've been extinct in the wild here for hundreds of years now, so I wouldn't worry too much about that, Joe,' Matt said. He looked reluctantly at the door of the ape house. I could see his old bike propped up outside. 'Better be heading off,' he said in a depressed voice. 'I need to be round the other side of the park in about five minutes flat. And there's a hill.'

5

Ivana Biscuit with Cheese

We couldn't get home fast enough on Friday afternoon.

'Did the bear and her cubs come?' I panted, crashing through the front door with Tori hot on my heels.

It was strange seeing Mum without Grandpa draped over her shoulder. Standing at the sink with a cup of coffee in her hand, she looked small and a bit lonely. Rabbit was sitting on her feet in a bid to get noticed. She woofed in greeting and got off Mum's shoes with a wag of her tail.

'Yes, they came,' Mum said.

'Can we see them?' I asked eagerly.

Mum shook her head. 'We must leave them alone until the mother bear wakes properly. Peace and quiet is very important in these early days.'

'We could go and look through the viewing window,' said Tori.

'We'll be really quiet,' I promised.

'Perhaps in the morning you can have a peep,' said Mum.

Her voice sounded funny. The light from the kitchen window caught the shine of tears on her cheeks.

'What's wrong?' I said in alarm. 'Is it Dad?'

Mum flushed at the mention of Dad's name. 'It's nothing. I'm just being silly. I'm missing Grandpa, perhaps.'

This was a clear case of a Mum Lie. She's not very good at lying – we can always tell. Plainly Dad had either called and they'd rowed, or he hadn't called and she was upset about it. Parents!

'Is Honey being a good mother?' Tori asked diplomatically.

Mum put her coffee down and hugged us both around the shoulders. 'Better than me, I think,' she said.

The phone rang and Mum was gone in a puff of dust, practically falling over Rabbit, who had now decided to lie across the kitchen door in that not-very-intelligent retriever way.

'She probably is missing Grandpa,' I said, staring at

the space where Mum had been. 'But I'll bet you anything she's missing Dad more.'

Out in the hall we could hear Mum's breathless 'Hello?' Without realizing it, I had gripped Tori's hand. We waited.

'Oh, hello, Jonas. Is everything OK with our bear and her cubs?'

Mum sounded as disappointed as we felt. No offence to Dr Nik or anything.

'Not Dad, then,' said Tori.

'Guess not,' I said gloomily.

The next day, Tori and I were up practically before the sparrows had taken their PJs off. It was dark outside, but the animals in the park were awake – you could hear them all calling. We dressed quickly.

'I'll make coffee for Mum if you wake her up,' said Tori, and headed down to the kitchen to boil the kettle. I could hear Rabbit's tail thumping eagerly on the kitchen floor at the prospect of an early-morning walk.

'Mum?' I peeped round Mum's door. 'Can we go and see the cubs now?'

Mum sat up blearily and rubbed her eyes. 'What?'

'You said we could see them in the morning,' I reminded her.

Mum looked exhausted. I noticed she had Dad's photo on the pillow beside her and quickly had to pretend I hadn't seen it.

'Is it morning?' she said in an attempt at making a joke. 'It feels like the middle of the night.'

'It's seven o'clock,' I said. Morning, right? Some parents are well lazy.

Ten minutes later, with Mum clutching her mug of Tori-made coffee, we were making our way through the frosty-looking park to the new bear enclosure by the tropical house. The nocturnal animals were still quite lively and the diurnal ones – that's the ones that hang about in the daytime – were starting to get up, meaning there was a lot of movement even in the pre-dawn light. Rabbit woofed, startling a pair of sleepy-eyed zebras.

Dr Nik came out of the bear house as we approached. He looked pale and tired, with bags big enough for a week's shopping under his dark eyes. He beamed when he saw us.

'Anita!' he exclaimed. He ruffled Rabbit's head. 'This is early. And the girls too!'

'We made her come,' Tori said.

'How is the bear?' I asked, desperate to know. 'How are her babies?'

Dr Nik gave a slow wink. 'You can come in and see for yourselves if you promise to be quiet. The bear house has been soundproofed, but we still need to be cautious. We tranquillized her just in case she woke up and became distressed, but the transfer went very well and she's hardly stirred at all, even though the sedative wore off hours ago. I have been monitoring her for most of the night in case of trouble.'

The new bear house was dim and cold, lit only with a single low-watt bulb to keep the mother bear calm and sleepy in her natural winter state. It took a little time for us to make out the shapes nestling in beside her big furry outline through the little viewing window. I counted: one, two, three.

'Bears usually have only one or two cubs,' said Dr Nik, seeing me counting. 'It's a sign that she was well looked after at the circus. Contented, well-fed animals tend to have bigger litters.'

I felt relieved. Circuses for wild animals were still all wrong, but at least this one had been run by people who knew how to look after a bear properly.

'What's her name?' Tori asked, staring at the sleeping animal.

'She probably had a name in the circus, but we don't know what it was,' said Dr Nik. He raised his eyebrows at us. 'Any ideas?'

'Brownie,' I said at once, before Tori could put her oar in. 'No – Belinda! Bella!'

'She's Russian,' Tori pointed out. 'Don't you think she needs a Russian name?'

'Moscow,' I said, quick as a flash. 'Cossack. Um . . .' What other Russian stuff could I think of?

'Those sound like boys' names,' Tori said. 'Anna, maybe?'

'We're at school with three Annas already,' I said. 'We've got to be more original than that. How about . . . Ivana?'

'Knock knock,' said Tori.

'What?' I said, thrown off for a minute.

'You heard,' said Tori.

'OK, who's there?'

'Ivana.'

'Ivana who?'

'Ivana biscuit.'

I groaned and smacked my forehead. 'That's majorly cheesy, Tori.'

Tori grinned. 'Ivana biscuit with cheese.'

OK. *That* was funny.

'Keep your voices down, *queridas*,' Mum warned.

'Ivana it is,' smiled Dr Nik we covered our mouths

with our hands. 'You can name the cubs when their mother is awake.'

Mum was watching the young bears carefully. 'They all seem to be feeding well,' she said.

'So far,' Dr Nik agreed. 'Let's hope things continue this way when the mother is awake and interacting with them. Her history of ill-temper may not make things easy.'

'Come back for some breakfast, Jonas,' Mum suggested. 'You look tired.'

'Remember what I said about Dr Nik liking Mum?' Tori said in a low voice as we followed the grown-ups out of the bear house. Mum was laughing at something Dr Nik was saying as they walked ahead of us towards our house with Rabbit shuffling along beside them. 'I wish I hadn't said it. It suddenly feels like maybe I've made something happen.'

'Don't worry,' I said as consolingly as I could. 'Guess what Mum was sleeping with when I went in to wake her up? *Dad's photo*. And remember how disappointed she sounded yesterday when it was Dr Nik on the phone and not Dad? Nothing's going to happen between her and Dr Nik, Tor.'

Tori chewed the side of her thumb. 'I don't

know,' she said. 'Look at them.'

I looked. They did look kind of cosy.

'We've got to get Mum and Dad back together as quickly as we can,' I said fervently. 'We're seeing Dad next weekend with the circus horses. We need a plan by then. OK?'

6

Hairdryer in the Dishwasher

The circus horses were every bit as beautiful as I'd imagined. The only disappointment was that they weren't wearing circus plumes on their heads.

'We keep their headpieces safe until they're in the ring,' laughed a strong girl with a gold stud in her nose, who was filling the horses' troughs with water. Dad was deep in conversation with Barney, the owner, in one corner of the yard. 'You didn't think they wore them all the time, did you?'

'If Taya was a circus horse, she'd wear hers all the time,' Tori said.

I blushed and pushed my cold hands a little deeper into my pockets. 'I so would not, Tori.'

Of course my sister was right. But don't tell her I told you so.

The horses were as interested in us as we were in them. They were all grey – every single one of them – and had these lovely dark eyes full of intelligence. I imagined them in the circus ring, trotting in time, their pale coats shining like polished silver in the twinkling lights of the Big Top. The air smelled of cool morning dew, warm sweating animals and the fresh hay-like pong of manure. I felt like I could stand here gazing at the horses all day, breathing them in like this.

'Do you ride them?' Tori asked as the girl with the nose stud poured out the last bucket of water into the horse trough at the end of the stable yard.

'Sometimes.' The girl carried her bucket back to a storage room and slung it inside before wiping her hands on her jodhpurs. 'But only in training, not in the ring. I'm not into performing myself. I'm Adriana, but call me Addie. Twins, are you?'

Tori and I introduced ourselves shyly.

'And your dad needs our horses for a film he's doing?'

'It's being directed by Pavlov Valkyrie,' said Tori with pride.

Addie whistled. 'Serious stuff then.'

Was I the only one round here who'd never heard of this Pavlov guy?

Dad came over, looking pleased. 'Barney and I just need to sort out a few details and we're through here, girls. Are you OK with Addie for a little while?'

'Could you get the horses to show us a trick, Addie?' I asked eagerly as Dad and Barney went into the stable office.

Addie smiled. 'I'm about to put Starlight through her paces in our covered arena. Want to come and watch?'

Daft question really.

Starlight was beautiful, with long slender legs and eyelashes practically as long as my nose. She snorted softly at us through velvety nostrils as Addie led her across the yard to the arena. Tori and I watched spellbound as she crisscrossed her legs and moved daintily sideways at Addie's instructions, then reared up on her hind legs to order. Her ears were pricked and alert and she held her tail up high with excitement as she went through her moves.

'She really enjoys it, doesn't she?' Tori said as Addie gave Starlight a treat and an affectionate rumple between her long ears at the end of what can only be described as a kind of one-horse ballet.

'Loves it.' Addie kissed the elegant grey horse on the nose.

'And it's not cruel making her do routines like that?' I asked cautiously, a mental image of Cash 'n' Carrie shimmering into my brain.

Addie smiled. I was relieved she hadn't taken offence. 'Certain animals thrive on the mental stimulation of performing. If Starlight didn't like it, she wouldn't do it. In the old days, it's true that people often used barbaric ways of training animals to do what they wanted – punishing them and so on. But the modern approach is to train by reward, not punishment. And of course there are lots of rules in place to protect performing animals today. Each case is different, but Starlight looks pretty happy to me. Wouldn't you say?'

Starlight nuzzled Addie's pocket, keen for another treat. Glancing around the well-kept arena, then out into the calm and spacious stable yard, I felt a bit silly for asking the question. It was important to judge things like circus animals on common sense, I decided, and common sense here was telling me that Addie was right.

Dad appeared at the door of the arena. 'Time to go, girls,' he said, blowing on his hands. It was a freezing day, a proper January shocker. 'The horses are booked for filming our circus scenes a week on Friday, up at Harting Park. Thanks very much for your time, Addie.'

As we left the arena, Tori and I both stroked Starlight's warm flank.

'See you in twelve days' time, Starlight,' I said, and the silver horse whickered at me like she knew exactly what I'd said.

'Right,' said Dad as we scooted along the motorway in our old black van towards the Fernleigh junction. 'Your mum's text said to drop you at the Kingfisher Centre bus stop for the two o'clock bus.' He checked his watch. 'We're in plenty of time.'

I took a deep breath. Tori and I had worked this out, down to the last detail. It was important that we didn't lose our nerve.

'Mum can't have meant the Kingfisher Centre,' I said as innocently as I could. 'The bus stop there is closed because of a road diversion.'

Dad frowned. 'I'm sure that's what the text said. Your mother doesn't usually get things like that wrong.'

'She's very tired at the moment,' I said. 'Looking after us by herself is hard work. We almost got dog food for supper last night.'

'Rabbit thought it was Christmas when Mum started scooping lasagne into her bowl,' Tori added.

'Oh, and she tried to put her hairdryer in the dishwasher yesterday too,' I said breezily. 'We caught her just in time.'

Dad looked alarmed. 'That sounds dangerous.'

'She's doing her best,' said Tori in her best and most reassuring voice. 'You mustn't worry, Dad. We shouldn't have said anything.'

As we had predicted, this made Dad look even more freaked. He frowned through his beard at us in the rear-view mirror. 'I think I should take you directly to Wild World and talk to your mother about how she's coping.'

'Dad, please don't.' I tried to say this in an off-putting way. 'Why don't you just drop us at the Brown Bell roundabout on your way through town? It's not that far to Wild World from there, and we only have to cross the dual carriageway once. I know the traffic lights are broken, but we've done it loads of times this week already.'

'Mum might really flip out at us if she thinks we've been complaining,' Tori said, wrapping things up as beautifully as a box of chocolates.

Dad thumped his foot on the accelerator. 'We'll

be there in ten minutes,' he said grimly. 'Your mother and I need to have a *serious* talk.'

Tori and I gave each other a silent low-five in the back seat. Phase One of the Masterplan was up and running.

7

A Bear, Not a Chihuahua

Unfortunately, Phase One was as far as the Masterplan got.

'What were you *thinking*?' Mum ranted at us. 'Telling your father all those lies! Now he believes I am not capable of looking after you and he will perhaps report me to the police! You are both banned – *banned* – from any after-school activities with your friends this week. You come straight back here where I can keep an eye on you!'

Tori and I sat miserably on the sofa, clutching Rabbit between us.

'We're sorry, Mum,' I mumbled.

'It was the only way we could think of getting you and Dad to talk to each other!' said Tori. 'All this texting and not talking is just *stupid*.'

Mum stood there with her hands on her hips, snorting and baring her teeth like a furious baboon. 'Well, we talked didn't we? Are you happy?'

'Shouted' was a more accurate description of what had happened when Dad confronted Mum in our kitchen. He had then stormed out of the house and down the garden with Mum hurling one of our new blue mugs at the back of his head. I'm pleased to say that it had missed and landed in the hedge, and was now safely back in the kitchen cupboard.

'It is not for you to tell me how to be with your father, Tori!' Mum yelled.

Tori jumped up, startling the already-nervous Rabbit into sliding off the sofa and padding away somewhere quieter. 'Well, someone's got to!' she yelled back. 'You sleep with Dad's picture. Taya told me. You still love him and you want him to come back. And he still loves you too. Why are you being so stubborn?'

'I . . .' Mum spluttered. 'It's . . .'

'Come on, Taya,' said Tori. 'We've got homework to do.'

I trailed after the blazing comet that was my sister.

'Good one,' I muttered as we reached our bedroom. 'As if Mum wasn't mad enough already.'

Tori shut the door with a bang. 'What would you have preferred me to say? Yes, Mum, no, Mum, three bags full, Mum?'

'No, but—'

'Thanks for backing me up, by the way,' she interrupted, giving me one of her most withering stares. 'Nice to know I've got your support.'

She marched over to her desk on the far side of the room and sat down, loudly shuffling her pencils and papers around so she could pretend she wasn't listening if I said anything. I considered my choices: watching telly within more-telling-off range of our furious mother, or doing my homework in the company of Icicle Girl.

I sat down at my desk and slowly pulled out my history book.

Being banned from doing stuff after school isn't too bad when you live in a wildlife park. The only problem was that Tori and I had to rely on each other for company instead of Joe or Biro or Cazza like normal. Being with someone who hates your guts twenty-four/seven isn't much fun, I can tell you that.

On Wednesday, Ivana the brown bear decided to wake up properly, improving Mum's mood. Since the bitterly cold day we'd spent with Dad and the circus horses, the weather had got much warmer – and it looked like Ivana's in-built spring detectors had kicked in.

'She's big, isn't she?' I said in awe as Ivana padded around her new enclosure, sniffing at things. She'd left her cubs in the dim quiet of the bear house, where Dr Nik and Mum were taking the opportunity to find out what sex they were and check they were healthy.

'She's a bear, not a chihuahua,' said Tori. 'Of course she's big.'

Ivana must have weighed something like three hundred kilos. Her coat was a glossy coffee-brown, with these lovely tufty ears and long claws on her feet. Her bottom was nicely padded, even after several months without food. I could totally see why teddy bears had been invented. If it hadn't been for her very fierce teeth, which I could see every time she yawned (she was still waking up, after all), I'd have wanted to give her a cuddle myself.

Dr Nik came out of the bear house with Mum. 'We've got two girls and a boy,' he announced with a smile. 'It looks like they've been feeding well, although the boy is smaller than I would like. Let's hope Ivana mothers them properly now she's truly awake.'

'Can we see them?' I asked eagerly. 'Can we name them?'

It was nearly six weeks since the bears had been born, and they'd reached a very cute stage with fuzzy brown fur all over their chunky bodies and their ears all neat and round and springing off their heads instead of lying flat against their skulls. They were clambering over each other in the bear house, squeaking crossly at the lack of milk while Ivana stretched her legs outside. The boy bear was easy to spot as he was quite a bit smaller than his sisters.

Tori got her way and named one of the girls Anna. 'And Sasha for the other one?' she said hopefully.

I would have preferred something a bit more fun, but seeing how I'd named Ivana I decided not to argue. Plus it was nice to have Tori talking to me again. 'What about the boy?' I said instead. 'Moscow or Cossack doesn't really fit with Anna and Sasha.'

'Ivan?'

'Too close to Ivana,' I said. 'Boris?'

The boy bear chose that moment to yawn. The beginnings of teeth gleamed in his small red mouth.

'Boris,' Tori agreed unexpectedly. 'He likes it.'

The bear house suddenly got darker as Ivana squeezed her furry bulk back through the door and flopped down on her straw bed again. Anna and Sasha were on her in moments, mewing and scrabbling at her belly with their little claws as they latched hungrily on to her teats.

'Where's Boris?' I said suddenly.

'I think Ivana just sat on him,' said Tori in panic.

We rushed out of the bear house.

'Dr Nik!'

'Mum!'

'Boris – the boy cub – just got squished!' we both shouted together.

Dr Nik hurried back into the bear house with Mum and us close behind him. 'It's very unlikely Ivana did that,' he began doubtfully, 'but he doesn't seem to be— Ah! There he is.'

Boris's furry face, his eyes so newly opened, had just appeared from underneath one of Ivana's big legs. He opened his mouth and gave a pathetic little squeak.

'Poor little thing!' I said, aghast at what it must have felt like having three hundred kilos of furry brown mum sitting on your head.

Boris shook his head to clear it. Then he inched his way along to join his sisters at Ivana's teats. The girls pushed him off with their scrabbling back legs. Grimly, Boris tried to scramble back towards the teats again as

Ivana shifted her bulk to a more comfortable position. The sudden movement dislodged the young bear and he fell back on the straw with a plop and a cry.

'He's very weak,' said Dr Nik with concern. 'It's possible that Ivana did injure him just now. Anita, we'd better keep a close eye.'

Mum and Dr Nik stayed in the bear house as we came back out into the sunshine. A couple of visitors to the park were looking at Ivana's new sign.

'"Eurasian Brown Bear, *Ursus arctos arctos*",' read one. 'Do you think it's from the Arctic, then?'

'Doesn't really matter, does it, since there's nothing here,' said the other, giving only half a glance at the empty enclosure. 'Anyway, it's not even rare.'

They moved on. Indignantly I made to chase after them and give them a few facts about how *arctos* comes from the Greek word for bear (I'd been doing some internet research) and how Ivana was just as interesting and important as the rarest creature at Wild World. Tori stopped me.

'Don't bother, Taya,' she said. 'Some people only see what they want to see.'

'Dr Nik's coming back with us for supper,' said Mum from behind us. She sounded happy. 'That's nice, isn't it?'

'What about seeing stuff you *don't* want to see?' I muttered to Tori as Dr Nik and Mum walked on ahead, a little too close together for comfort.

'Not much we can do about that either,' Tori said grimly.

8

A Different Tin of Sardines

Dr Nik came for dinner three times in the next four days.

'He's practically got a peg with his name on it at the front door,' Tori muttered on Sunday evening as Dr Nik smiled goodnight at us, kissed Mum on both cheeks, and vanished into the night. Mum had looked a little flushed and started humming in a distracted way while she loaded the dishwasher.

'They've mainly been talking about whether or not Boris needs fostering,' I said. 'That's hardly the stuff of romance.'

'It's all about reading between the lines, Taya,' said Tori darkly.

Most of Mum and Dr Nik's conversation *had* been

about the bear situation. Now she was properly awake, Ivana's reputation for having a bad temper sadly seemed to be true – and Boris *had* been hurt when she sat on him. But who was I kidding? Even I'd noticed that Dr Nik had started steering things in a more personal direction.

'We're seeing Dad tomorrow after school up at Harting Park,' I reminded Tori as we trudged upstairs to our room. 'Perhaps we can talk to him about it.'

'He'll probably just think we're setting him up again,' Tori said glumly. 'I don't think Dad's ever going to believe another word we say.'

'He'll have forgiven us by now,' I said, sounding more confident than I felt. 'And Harting Park should be awesome anyway. You'll meet your precious Pavlov Volderol.'

'*Valkyrie*,' Tori corrected with a tut. 'Do you really think we will?'

'Dad's got to talk to him about the circus horse scene,' I said. 'He won't leave us sitting in the van, will he?'

Tori flashed me a nervous smile. 'Pavlov Valkyrie's famously scary. I don't know if I'm looking forward to meeting him for real or not.'

'He can't be much scarier than Mum last weekend,' I

said. 'Thank wombats this week is over, Tor. Our mates have probably forgotten we exist and we'll be back to Social Square One. Things have *got* to start improving around here or I'll go nuts.'

'You're already halfway there,' said Tori. 'But that's just the way you're made. Hey! That pillow nearly took my eye out!'

Don't tell me you wouldn't have done the same.

At school Joe was full of questions as usual.

'Are they really cute, the cubs?' he asked as we walked to our art lesson. 'Is your mum going to foster the one you said got injured? Can I come and see them this week?'

'Ivana's been pretty grumpy and distracted since waking up,' I said. '*All* the cubs are struggling now, but Boris most of all. Because he hurt his leg, he doesn't get to her teats quickly enough to get much of a feed before she gets up and starts pacing around the enclosure again. Bear cubs may be a whole lot bigger than puppies, but they're just as vulnerable if their mother neglects them.'

'Does that mean your mum might foster all *three*?' Joe gasped. 'That's *so* awesome!'

Cazza snorted beside Tori. 'Watch them chairs and

beds and porridge, yeah?'

'Call me Goldilocks and you're dead,' said Tori. But her face twitched as she said it so I knew she didn't really mean it. It was pretty funny actually by Cazza's standards.

'How do you like your porridge, Goldilocks?' Cazza did this great bellow of laughter that made me think of a hungry hyena.

Joe suddenly stopped. 'My book bag,' he said anxiously. 'I left it in the form room.'

'We don't need our bags for art,' I said.

'I have to go and get it.' Joe's voice got a bit higher. 'Really, I have to. Come with me, Taya? Please?'

'But we'll be late!' I objected.

Joe genuinely looked like he was going to cry. 'I need it, Taya!'

Tori shrugged at me and kept walking with Caz and some others.

'Blimey, Joe – you and that bag!' I said, perplexed. 'What have you got in there that's so precious?'

Joe swallowed. 'A picture of Mum. I carry it around so she can see what I'm doing. Well, not *see* exactly,' he amended a little sheepishly, 'because she's in the bag. But it means she's wherever I am, so I think she sort of knows.'

I stared at him. He stared back, his Adam's apple bobbing up and down like a nervous ping-pong ball.

Joe's mum had walked out on him and his dad three years earlier. In private Tori and I had a lot of theories about where she'd gone and why. It was just *weird*, the way she'd left without a word. What mother goes off and leaves her nine-year-old kid behind without any explanations? He never talked about her, but the fact that Joe carried his mum's picture around everywhere he went . . . Well. It explained a lot about Joe Morton.

'Of course we'll get your bag, mate,' I said, recovering. 'We'll only be a couple of minutes late. Come on.'

Dad collected us after school and took us off to his meeting with Tori's hero, Pavlov Thingamajig. Dad was still pretty mad at us for setting up him and Mum, but luckily his mind soon switched to his job and the subject of flung mugs and broken traffic lights was dropped.

As we swung in through the curly iron gates of Harting Park, we glimpsed a gorgeous black carriage standing by the great front door of the house with two gleaming chestnut horses strapped in between the shafts. It was like going back in time a hundred and thirty years – provided you didn't look at all the filming trucks, cameras, massive lights, fluffy grey microphones on sticks, electricity generators, and snaky black cables everywhere.

'Oh!' I said, entranced. 'A proper old-fashioned horse carriage! Tori, look!'

Tori's face was glued to the other window, where a group of people were standing in a huddle by a set of long French windows.

'That's Pavlov Valkyrie!' Tori hissed. 'There! In the middle! There!'

All I saw was an oldish geezer with a shock of silver-white hair and a great beak of a nose standing in the middle of the group. He looked like an elderly eagle.

'Not really heartthrob material is he?' I said in disappointment.

Dad parked, jumped out of the car, and strode towards the huddle. We hurried after him, pulling our school coats around us. It was cold again today and the early February sun was already beginning to set. What little colour there was to begin with had started to ooze away into greyness, apart from the bits that were lit up with huge arc lights like a massive great stage set – which of course it was.

I thought I'd got used to all the razzamatazz that

goes with filming stuff: all the people, and the bustle, and the crackle of walkie-talkies. But then I realized that a movie was a different tin of sardines. It was everything we'd seen before times about a hundred, with extra bells and whistles and people scurrying about carrying odd bits of equipment. A lady stood by one of the side doors in a full pink dress and large hat with a black feather in it, smoking a fag and playing with her iPad while people crouched at her hem and sewed up a bit of trailing petticoat. One of the horses between the carriage shafts snorted and produced a pile of manure, which was hurriedly removed and the gravel on the driveway carefully pushed back to exactly how it was before.

As Tori and I gawked at everything, a tall black guy with a head full of dreadlocks peeled away from the group gathered around the director and came to meet us with a meaty hand extended in Dad's direction.

'Andy Wild, right? Dave Sutton, great to meet you. Good news on our circus horses. Mr Valkyrie's got everything worked out down to the tiniest detail, as usual, so he shouldn't keep you long. He just wants to talk you through scene essentials on Friday.'

Dave looked a little frightened when he said the

director's name. Beside me Tori giggled in a seriously un-Tori way.

'My daughters – Taya and Tori,' said Dad, gesturing at us as he shook Dave's hand. 'It's their first film set.'

Yours too, Dad, I felt like saying, but didn't.

The group around Mr Valkyrie parted like someone had just run a comb down the middle and the eagle-beaked guy stepped forward. Dave made a cringy little bow that made me think of a maid bobbing a curtsey at a king.

'Mr Valkyrie, this is Andy Wild from Wild About Animals – the guy who's organized your circus horses.'

Dad's hand was gripped in a large pair of hands with hairy grey backs.

'I must congratulate you,' said Pavlov Valkyrie, in a voice that was part American and part something else – Russian, maybe. 'Finding Kurdish circus horses at month's notice in England! You are magician, my friend.'

I noticed the way he didn't say 'a' or 'the' about half a second before I noticed the colour draining from Dave and Dad's faces. Dad cleared his throat.

'Er – *Kurdish* circus horses, Mr Valkyrie?'

9

Snow in a Microwave

Right there and then, I understood why everyone was so scared of Pavlov Valkyrie. He drew his beetly grey eyebrows together and his whole face changed from a wrinkly-but-moderately-friendly eagle to something closer to an ultra-aggressive vulture. Dave Sutton looked ready to faint. The gaggle around him melted away like snow in a microwave.

'Yes,' the director said, in a voice quieter than a room full of mice in tiny cotton slippers. 'Kurdish circus horses. You have Kurdish circus horses for me.'

'No, Mr Valkyrie,' Dad said, swallowing. Instinctively Tori and I stood a bit closer to him. 'I have plain English circus horses. Six fine greys. I was told—'

'KURDISH HORSES!' shouted the director so loudly that the normal horses in the carriage shafts by the front door both started. 'Of COURSE it is Kurdish horses! The whole STORY is about love affair between English lady and Kurdish horseman, so we must have KURDISH HORSES!'

'I didn't know Kurdish horses were different from normal horses,' stuttered Dave. His dreadlocks were practically whistling back off his head like in one of those cartoons when someone's really shouting, 'It—'

'I have gone to great expense to source finest Kurdish actor of his generation, Mirza Khan! Now I discover I don't have Kurdish horses? But it is disaster! DISASTER!' the director screamed. 'Are you imbecile not to know difference between Kurdish horse and other horse?'

'There aren't many people who'd know the difference, Mr Valkyrie,' said Dave in a final desperate attempt to save his head from being removed from his shoulders. 'Surely you can make an exception here, given our time constraints? We film Mr Wild's horses and—'

Beside me Tori winced. I remembered what she'd said about Mr Stickler For Detail Valkyrie.

'GET OUT OF MY SIGHT!' shrieked Pavlov

Valkyrie, before launching into this volley of no doubt extremely rude Russian, or wherever he was from. Dave did as he was told, extremely quickly.

'"Not many people know difference",' the old director muttered, breathing hard. Someone appeared at his elbow and placed a large cup of black coffee in his hand as it clutched convulsively at the air. '*I* know difference! Do *you* know difference?'

He whirled round at Dad, who was too paralysed to speak.

'Yes, he does, Mr Valkyrie,' squeaked Tori.

Pavlov Valkyrie's eyebrows beetled up into his hair. So did mine. How did my twin have the guts to say anything at all to this tornado person?

'He's a professional wildlife photographer, Mr Valkyrie.' Tori's voice was steadying now. 'I bet he can tell the difference between Kurdish horses and other ones as easily as black and white. It's just no one told him they had to be Kurdish.'

The director stared hard at Dad. Dad took an involuntary step backwards. He trod on my toe, but I was too scared to shout out.

'Kurdish circus horses by Friday,' said the old eagle quietly. 'Save my fiasco, Mr Wild. Go and do this for my film.'

'Er,' Dad croaked. 'Er, OK. Friday. Good as done, Mr Valkyrie.'

I hadn't seen Mum this concerned about Dad since before everything went wrong. That had to be good, right? Even though Dad had to get up to his neck in scary trouble to achieve it.

'Your poor father!' she exclaimed over and over as Tori and I recounted our catastrophic afternoon, with extra details to make the most of Mum's anxiety. 'Oh Andy! How will he do it? Kurdish horses in Surrey? In four days' time? And Pavlov Valkyrie's film a disaster if he fails? Oh!'

'He's gutted.' I allowed a little pause for an image of a gutted Dad to float into Mum's head before turning the screw. 'You saw him for yourself. As white as a very scared sheet.'

Mum's eyes flew to the kitchen door and we knew she was remembering Dad all pale and trembling with the shock of having taken on the world's most impossible job as he dropped us off and hurried away into the darkness to contemplate his impending death on Friday.

'And I feel like it's all my fault,' Tori muttered. 'If I hadn't said that about Dad knowing the difference—'

'You had to say something,' I interrupted. 'Dad was frozen to the spot! And anyway, it's true that Dad knows about horses. He's photographed plenty galloping around Africa and Siberia and everywhere. It was your scary director who decided that meant Dad could actually *find* some by Friday.'

Mum's eyes glistened on cue. She cuddled the snoozing Boris up close, and it wasn't clear who was comforting whom.

Boris had been rescued that afternoon following a nasty incident with Ivana almost biting him. Sasha and Anna had been judged big enough now to stick up for themselves – at least until Dr Nik and Mum could figure out what Ivana's problem was. Boris's leg was still sore, and he was desperately hungry. He'd taken a huge feed of milk and, to Rabbit's complete and utter joy, had fallen asleep in her basket with his bandaged leg sticking up in the air. Then Mum had yelped in shock about Dad's Mission Impossible and woken him up. He was already pretty heavy, but we'd all taken turns to cuddle him; his fur smelled musky and milky. Rabbit sat on her big yellow bottom by the table leg and drooled up at the bear now nestled in the crook of Mum's arm. She's all mother, that dog.

'Maybe Dad'll find the right horses,' I said

uncertainly. 'He's got loads of contacts.'

'Maybe he can find some horses that *look* like Kurdish horses and trick Pavlov Valkyrie into filming them,' Tori said.

At that point I realized just how bad things were for Dad if even *Tori* was kidding herself with fairy tales about pulling the wool over her hero's eagly eyes. I felt wistful as I thought about Starlight. It was sad that we wouldn't be seeing her again after all.

Boris gave a snort and a cry. Rabbit whined hopefully as the young bear cub opened his bright black eyes.

'Hello, Boris,' said Tori, switching her attention to our newest member of the family. 'How long do you think you'll have to keep him away from Ivana, Mum?'

Mum stroked Boris between the ears. He yawned. 'It's critical that we keep him long enough for his leg to heal. If we put him back too soon, he won't have a chance back in the enclosure – especially with Ivana and her bad temper.'

Tori looked troubled. 'You mean, he'd die?'

'Yes, I'm afraid he would,' said Mum gently. 'We should perhaps have let nature take its course, but . . . I couldn't see him suffering. Not when I am the one who arranged for Ivana and her family to come to Wild World.' Now it was her turn to look troubled. 'Did I do the right thing, *queridas*?'

Tori and I both gazed at Boris. The sleeping bear with his bandaged leg looked really vulnerable, even though he was the size of our sitting-room pouffe.

'Of course you did, Mum,' I said stoutly. 'We'll keep him until his leg's better and Ivana will have chilled out and everything will be *fine*.'

Mum sighed. 'This is not just about Boris's leg. I wish we could work out the problem with Ivana. She just paces around all day long, ignoring the cubs or being aggressive with them. If this continues we may have to take Anna and Sasha too, even though their legs are OK.'

'Ivana must have been more traumatized by her life in the circus than we realized,' I said, feeling worried for the mother bear. Even though she'd been well fed and apparently looked after OK, what other explanation could there be?

'Perhaps.' Mum rubbed her eyes. 'But we have to find the answer soon or two more cubs will become motherless as well. I hope I have not taken on too much.'

I thought of Dad. 'If you have, you're not the only one,' I said.

10

Goddle Waddle Godalming

Biro was drawing horses again.

'*Le cheval*,' said Joe helpfully.

Biro looked up, his eyes glazed like he'd been somewhere else for a while.

'What you've drawn,' Joe went on. He pointed at Biro's horse. '*Le cheval*.'

'MORTON!' roared Mr Jones, making everyone jump with sheer terror. '*Pas un mot plus!*' Our Welsh French teacher, or Wench teacher for short, has two volume settings: *fort* (loud) and *très fort* (louder).

'What's "pazza mow ploo" mean?' whispered Cazza as the class cowered over their books.

'Not another word,' I whispered back. I actually quite like French, even though Mr Jones scares me

69

nearly as much as Pavlov Valkyrie does.

'All right, twin-face,' Cazza snarled, offended. 'Keep your greasy hair on.'

No one said anything else for the rest of the lesson – apart from Tosh, when Mr Jones threw him out of the class for carving a rude French word he'd found in his dictionary into his desk. Cash 'n' Carrie – Heather Cashman and Carrie Taylor – joined Tosh for giggling about it. I won't print the word Tosh carved but I'm quite surprised Mr Jones didn't throw him out of the window instead of the door.

'You're good at drawing horses, Biro,' said Joe, slinging his bag over his shoulder as the bell went and we all breathed without fear of being screamed at.

Biro shrugged a pleased kind of shrug. 'My uncle has horses.'

I stopped. Tori bumped into me with a muttered: 'Taya, you wazz!'

'Biro,' I said, struck by the glorious possibility that suddenly lay before me. 'You're Kurdish, aren't you?'

Biro had come to England from Iraq a year earlier, but was Kurdish not Iraqi. His people lived in the joined-up corners of a whole bunch of countries like Iraq, Iran, Syria and Turkey but had no actual country of their own.

Biro nodded.

'And is your uncle Kurdish too?'

Biro nodded again. He prefers body language to the verbal kind.

Tori was alert now. 'I don't suppose . . .' she said.

'I guess it's stupid to ask, but . . .' I said.

'Are his *horses* Kurdish?' we both asked together.

For a third extraordinary time, Biro's chin dipped towards the floor and up again.

'Oh my wombats!' I gasped. I grabbed Biro by both arms. 'And is . . . are . . . I guess there's no way on this earth that your uncle's horses are in England?'

'They are in Godalming,' said Biro, like a bunch of Kurdish horses in the Surrey Hills were the most normal thing in the entire world.

'*Godalming?*' I said. Godalming was about twenty minutes from Fernleigh and half an hour from Harting Park.

'Your uncle's horses are in *Godalming*?' said Tori, just to be sure we weren't hearing things.

'Godalming, OK? He said Godalming!' Cazza said irritably. 'Goddle Waddle Godalming.' She stopped, looking distracted. 'Godalming sounds weird when you say it a whole load of times. Godalming. Godalming. Freaky.'

'Biro, listen very carefully,' I said, tripping over my tongue in my excitement. 'Do you think your uncle would be interested in renting his horses out to make a film?'

'It's a Pavlov Valkyrie film,' Tori added reverently. 'He'll pay your uncle lots of cash.'

Biro looked mystified. 'A film? Yes, maybe. You want that I call him?'

'Yes! Yes, we do!' said Tori, as I started capering about like a Kurdish horse whose tail's on fire. 'Can you call him now? Our dad's supposed to find some Kurdish horses for this film the day after tomorrow and we didn't think . . . Anyway if you could call him and if he said yes it would save our Dad's life completely and utterly.'

'Kurdish horses in Godalming!' I squealed, still capering.

Biro pulled a little phone out of his bag. 'Give me one minute, OK?'

When he came to fetch us from school, Dad's grin was so broad it practically wrapped around the whole of his head. He gave me and Tori whopping great hugs, but saved the pick-you-up-off-the-floor hug for Biro.

'I can't tell you how grateful I am to your uncle for

this, son,' he said, putting the frantically blushing Biro back on the ground again. 'Kurdish horses twenty minutes from here! They're such wonderful animals. I photographed them in Syria many years ago, but I never thought I'd see them again.'

'They are pure Kurdish horses, Mr Wild,' Biro said as we all piled into Dad's van. 'My uncle breeds them for many years. We are very proud of our horses. I ride them all my life with my cousins. What is this film?'

'It's called *The Rose and the Ring*,' said Dad.

'It's about a lady called Rose de Lacey who falls in love with a Kurdish circus horseman and, like I said, it's directed by this completely well-known director called Pavlov Valkyrie,' said Tori enthusiastically. 'It's a true story from more than a hundred years ago.'

'Who is the actor for the horseman?' Biro asked. 'He is Kurdish?'

'Someone called Mirza Khan,' I put in, determined to be a part of this conversation.

'*Mirza Khan?*' Biro said in disbelief. 'But with my people, he is *famous*.'

'Mr Valkyrie – the director – tends to get the best,' Dad replied.

Biro started chatting at full speed in his own language, before remembering that we couldn't understand him. 'I am excited,' he explained breathlessly.

'We guessed,' I grinned, and high-fived Tori across the back seat.

Biro's uncle Ardalan lived in a gigantic house tucked away in a secret little valley beyond Godalming. The whole place seemed to be covered in gold. Gold doorknobs, gold window frames, gold fringes on the curtains and the rugs. Through tall windows with gold window fittings, I could see a field sloping away to some trees and a collection of horses grazing quietly around the edges.

An older version of Biro appeared at the top of the stairs with his arms held out and a wide smile on his face. The gold teeth in Uncle Ardalan's mouth matched his house.

'My uncle speaks no English,' Biro explained as the older man kissed Dad firmly on both cheeks and pinched my and Tori's chins between rough fingers that smelled of dark, sweet tobacco. 'But he is very happy to show his horses to you and bring them for your film on Friday – if you want them.'

Biro went into a stream of noise with his uncle in which I picked out the words 'Mirza Khan'. His uncle looked quite agitated and pumped Dad's hand hard as we walked down the drive to the field.

Six horses galloped up to say hello over the fence. They were neat little things, more the size of ponies than horses, with high swishing tails and flaring nostrils. They came in a mix of different colours.

Biro's uncle began speaking his liquid language. Biro translated.

'The Kurdish horse is one of the oldest breed of horses. He's quite small, you see? Kurdish horses are only a metre and a half tall, or sometimes smaller. They are very strong and useful for travelling in mountains – we have a lot of mountains in Iraq. People say that the Kurdish horse is the father of all thoroughbred horses in the world today. The Kurdish people love their horses like children, so in the past they were not very good in battles because the people were scared if their horses get hurt.'

That was nice, I thought. Thinking more about your horses' welfare than whether you were going to win a battle or not.

As Biro's uncle excused himself and went off with his phone stuck to his ear, we fussed over the horses and rubbed their velvet noses. They enjoyed our attention, pushing at our hands for more stroking, and sniffing hopefully at our sleeves in case we'd stashed a bunch of secret apples up there. They were wilder-looking than Starlight – I could easily picture them all charging around the mountains of Iraq.

Biro's uncle came striding back towards us, surrounded by four excitable dark-haired young men.

'My cousins,' said Biro. He looked eager. 'My uncle tells them about the film. Do you think it is possible for us to be in Mr Valkyrie's film with our horses, Mr Wild? To ride with Mirza Khan . . .'

'Well . . .' Dad began.

Biro's cousins surrounded us before Dad managed to finish that particular thought. They slapped Biro on the back and pinched his cheeks and rumpled his hair, saying 'Hi, how's it going?' to us and Dad in perfect English. Then suddenly they all vaulted over the fence into the field. Biro's uncle clicked his fingers at Biro, who scrambled into the field as well.

'What are they going to do?' asked Tori in fascination.

'I think they're going to show us some Kurdish horsemanship,' said Dad.

Biro and his family jumped on to the horses and began to ride them bareback. The horses were so little that, without stirrups, the riders' feet practically touched the ground. The air was filled with joking and shouting as the horses wheeled around and charged up and down, one or two of them giving cheeky little rears and prompting extra cheering from the other riders. We watched Biro flying across the field, his face so low over his horse that its mane blew back into his eyes.

Biro's uncle suddenly gave a piercing whistle and the horses stopped dead in their tracks.

'Unbelievable,' I said in amazement as each horse started walking slowly and daintily *backwards*, guided only by Biro's uncle's whistling and what looked like a fair bit of concentration from the cousins.

Dad's fingers were shaking as he took out his phone.

'Mr Valkyrie, please. It's Andy Wild, from Wild About Animals. The horse guy, yes . . . Mr Valkyrie? I have your Kurdish horses. And I may have a group of Kurdish riders too, if you need them. You do? Excellent! See you on Friday!'

11

Singing in that Wuffly Way

'Come in, Dad,' Tori begged as Dad swung into the Wild World car park. 'Mum would really like to see you. Please?'

'I'd better not,' Dad began, looking twitchy.

I held up a fierce finger. 'Who just saved your neck and made your name as the Animal Guy Who Can Find Any Animal in Two Days Flat?'

'Who just made sure that you're now friends for life with one of the world's most respected film directors?' Tori added.

'You *totally* owe us,' I said.

'All right!' Dad protested. 'But don't blame me if your mother chucks another bit of crockery at my head, OK?'

The house was dark, lit only by the porch light as we approached. My heart sank. A golden opportunity for Mum and Dad to talk to each other – and Mum wasn't in. Our only encouragement was that Dad was clearly just as disappointed as we were.

'She probably won't be long,' I said as Tori unlocked the front door.

'Come in and wait,' Tori begged.

Dad looked unsure. He thumbed back in the direction of the van. 'I should probably be getting on—'

'Andy?'

Mum was coming towards us through the gloom with Rabbit waddling at her side. Her hair was plaited untidily over one shoulder and Boris was snuggled in her arms, his bandaged leg sticking out sideways.

'Hi, Anita,' said Dad awkwardly. He bent down to stroke Rabbit's ears.

The air turned stodgy. What had seemed like a good idea now felt like a terrible one. Tori rushed inside at top speed in case there were missiles.

'The girls found me some Kurdish horses,' Dad said at last, as Rabbit practically tried to climb into his trousers with delight at seeing him.

'I know,' Mum said.

'Riders too. An added bonus. Mr Valkyrie's so

pleased he's doubled my fee.'

Mum looked genuinely pleased. 'I'm glad.'

She carried Boris into the house. I made faces at Dad, urging him to follow. Dad pushed the delirious Rabbit out of the way and obeyed.

'So,' he said as we reached the kitchen. 'The young bear. A new fostering project for you, the girls tell me.'

'Mum's well pleased to see Dad,' Tori said to me in a low voice as, with a few creaks and rusty squeals the conversation train finally started to roll between our parents. 'Look at her face. Gooey as chocolate cake.'

'I think that's for Boris.'

I didn't say this because I thought Tori was wrong but because I was keen to protect myself from disappointment. My eyes flicked to the kitchen cupboard where the mugs were kept.

'Gorgeous, isn't he?' Mum was saying as Dad stroked the cub's head. Rabbit started singing in that wuffly way she has when life has just become unbearably good for a dog. 'His leg is beginning to heal now. Unfortunately we think we'll have to take his sisters tomorrow as well. The mother bear is either aggressive with them or ignores them completely.'

'Bears can be difficult animals,' Dad said. He cleared

his throat. 'Has, er, Jonas Nikolaides got any ideas about why she's behaving like that?'

'None,' Mum admitted.

Dad suddenly got bold. 'I'm not expected on set with the horses until Friday, so I'm free tomorrow afternoon. Shall I come over and help?'

Mum stared at him over the top of Boris's woolly brown head. 'I don't know what you can do,' she said after a moment.

Oh *wombats*, I thought. Mum just went and burst the balloon.

'But you might surprise me,' Mum added. She smiled.

Dad's chest swelled up like a pigeon's. 'Well, I'm not the Animal Guy for nothing, you know.'

'I never said you were.'

Rabbit let out a terrible fart, somewhat spoiling the moment.

'Tomorrow then,' said Dad, backing out of the kitchen as we all waved our hands in front of our noses and Rabbit retreated to her basket. 'By the bear house? I'll pick the girls up from school and bring them right over.'

Tori and I didn't hear Mum's reply because we'd fled up the stairs to squeal into our pillows.

* * *

Dad had spruced himself up a bit when he collected us from the school gates the next day. His beard looked like he'd given it a bit of a trim and he was wearing a nice blue-and-white checked shirt that I'd never seen before.

'New shirt, Dad?' said Tori.

Dad fiddled a bit with his collar. 'Yes. No. Can't remember,' he said shiftily. 'What news from your mother? About the bears?'

'Not very good,' I told him. 'They had to tranquillize Ivana this morning so she'd stop pacing around and lie down for long enough to let Anna and Sasha have a feed. They were starving.'

Although it's never very nice having to take babies away from their mothers, Tori and I both agreed that Boris had a better deal than his sisters just now, even with a bandage on his leg.

Dad changed gear. 'She was a circus bear, wasn't she?'

'Yes, poor thing,' said Tori with feeling.

'Is it possible that she's missing her circus life?'

This was such an odd thing to say that Tori and I were both speechless for a second.

'*Missing* it?' I said at last. 'She's a wild animal, Dad. If anything she'd be missing the wild.

She's totally traumatized.'

'Do you know for sure she was captured from the wild, not raised in captivity?'

Tori and I glanced at each other. No, we didn't know that for sure.

Dad went on. 'Animals like their habits. Certain food, favourite places, particular ways of behaviour. When I was photographing them in the wild, I researched their habits first to make sure of catching them in the right place at the right time. If Ivana has spent her entire life in captivity, she would most likely be the same.'

'Being made to do what the circus owner wants?' Tori demanded. 'Being kept in a cage instead of a natural, open space? Sure she's missing that, Dad.'

'Your mother said she was in good condition when she arrived at Wild World,' Dad pointed out. 'And she had three cubs, didn't she? A sign that she was pretty well nourished and cared for, in my experience. Of course I'm not saying wild animals in circuses should be encouraged—'

'Good!' I said in outrage.

'I'm just saying that each case should be judged individually,' Dad finished.

Dad's words made me think of Addie, the girl who

looked after Starlight. She'd said something similar about circus animals. *Each case is different.* And, more interestingly: *Certain animals thrive on the mental stimulation of performing.*

'What do you think Ivana did in her circus?' asked Dad.

We both shrugged, still taking in the weird possibility that Dad was on to something.

'Bears can be taught all sorts of tricks,' he said, drumming his fingers on the steering wheel as he thought. 'Tightrope-walking, for instance.'

'You think we should put a tightrope up in Ivana's enclosure?' said Tori disbelievingly.

The signs for Wild World were coming up on the right. 'Isn't it worth a try?' Dad said as he put his indicator on. 'For the sake of Ivana's mental health – and the lives of her cubs?'

'That is the craziest thing I've ever heard!' exclaimed Dr Nik at the bear house fifteen minutes later. He hadn't looked very pleased to see Dad.

'Jonas, he could be right,' said Mum. She stroked Boris, who was cuddled in her arms as usual. 'What harm could it do?'

Dad looked at the ground, most likely trying to hide

a satisfied smile that Mum was agreeing with him.

Dr Nik began pacing around. 'This is a place of science, research and conservation – not a place for animals to perform! Imagine the uproar if we were seen to encourage Ivana in something so unnatural!'

'Maybe she *likes* performing,' I said. 'Maybe that's the whole point.'

We all looked at poor Ivana as she paced up and down, up and down, looking for whatever she was looking for. There was a pathetic mewing sound from the bear house as Anna and Sasha begged her to come back to them. Boris squirmed restlessly in Mum's arms.

Dr Nik blew out his cheeks. 'OK,' he said reluctantly. 'Let's see if we can get Ivana back into the bear house for a while so we can set this thing up.'

Ivana was coaxed into the bear house with a box of apples, slumping down on the straw. Anna and Sasha fell on her hungrily. Dr Nik shut the door and called maintenance.

'Don't argue,' he warned as the two burly maintenance men looked wide-eyed at the request for a tightrope to install in the enclosure. 'I'm struggling with the idea myself.'

As the guys fetched a length of thick rope and started fixing it to two low poles in the enclosure, Tori and I started giggling. It would be too weird if this actually worked.

'I never thought I'd see the day when I was giving a bear a bit of rope to practise a balancing act on,' Dr Nik said. He looked depressed at the way Mum and Dad were standing quite close together. 'If you're wrong about this, I'll never be able to hold my head up in professional circles again.'

12

Totally Crazy Bananas

There was an exciting moment as Ivana came shambling out of the reopened bear house and sniffed at her new toy. But then she simply scratched her back against one of the holding poles and headed off to the far side of the enclosure, not giving the tightrope another glance. A magpie fluttered in and sat on it for a while, fluffing out its ink and snow feathers, before zooming off in horror as Ivana came pacing past again with her big brown bulk swaying from side to side.

Dr Nik looked thunderous.

'Perhaps we should give it a couple of days,' I said feebly. 'She won't have seen a tightrope in a while.'

Ivana paced along her well-worn route. Daylight was

fading and the park lights had just flicked on. Who were we fooling? This just wasn't going to happen.

Matt came puffing up, his bike wobbling from side to side on his approach. As he swerved towards us he almost took out one of the maintenance men, who'd stuck around for a laugh.

'Novel idea, Jonas,' he said breathlessly, dismounting. 'What's next? Jugglers? Oh, hello, Andy – good to see you.'

Dr Nik looked even more cheesed off.

'It wasn't Dr Nikolaides' idea,' Dad confessed. 'It was mine.'

Matt mopped his forehead. 'It's not a bad one. A bit unorthodox, but we're at the point where we'll try anything. Is she interested?'

Everyone shook their heads silently and Matt looked disappointed.

I almost took off as I felt Ivana's hot bear breath on my neck. She'd come right up to the fence and was staring at us, her nose only a couple of centimetres away.

'Hey, Ivana,' I said, trying to control my breathing, which had flipflopped all over the place. 'Tightrope-walking not your thing, then?'

Ivana made an extraordinary sound. It was like a

groan, booming deep down in her belly.

'I think Ivana just understood what I said,' I said in wonder. 'Can bears speak English?'

'I think Chinese is more their thing,' said Tori sarcastically.

Ivana groaned at us again. It was the most tragic sound I'd ever heard. In Mum's arms, Boris made a smaller, lighter version of the same noise.

'What's she looking at Matt for?' Tori asked, following the bear's sad black gaze.

'Perhaps I smell like dinner,' Matt joked.

'I don't think she's looking at Matt,' I said. A tiny little seed of an idea was starting to unfurl leaves in my head. 'I think she's looking at his bike.'

The big brown bear's eyes were fixed steadily on Matt's bicycle. Suddenly I didn't need to share a language with Ivana to understand what she wanted. It was *obvious*.

'She wants to ride it,' I shouted. 'That's her trick! That's her circus thing! She's stopped pacing, hasn't she? She's found what she's been looking for! She's been looking for a *bicycle*!'

Mum and Dad looked astonished. Matt and Dr Nik both looked like someone had hit them hard with a pair of smelly haddocks.

'But—'

I grabbed Matt's bicycle. 'Put this in Ivana's enclosure,' I insisted. 'What have you got to lose?'

Ivana was coaxed back into the bear house with difficulty and the door was shut.

'I can't believe I'm giving my bike to a bear,' said Matt, unlocking the side gate that led into the enclosure and wheeling his bicycle inside. 'It's a good job it's an old one.'

The maintenance men took the opportunity to dismantle the tightrope and take down the holding poles as Matt propped his two-wheeler up against a rock near the middle. A crowd of curious spectators started to gather around the edges of the bear house as the gate was locked again and Matt rejoined us.

'Anita?' he said to Mum. 'It's show time. Let her out, will you?'

'This is even madder than the tightrope idea,' said Tori, while Mum carefully handed Boris to Dad and rushed off to open the bear-house door.

'Totally crazy bananas!' I said gleefully.

There was a moment of hush as the bear-house door slid open and Ivana came out. She made straight for the bike, trotting in her hurry to reach it.

'Now I've seen it all,' Dr Nik breathed as the bear calmly took the handlebars and climbed aboard, pedalling around her enclosure in a perfect circle.

'It was *incredible*!' Tori enthused to Cazza at registration the next day. Joe and Biro were listening hard as well, their eyes goggling. So were Cash 'n' Carrie, but they were pretending not to. 'She started pedalling and didn't stop for ages. And then when she did, she trotted quietly into the bear house and let her cubs feed on her for ages, like a perfect mother.'

'Maybe I should put *my* mum on a bike and send her round our living room a couple of times a day,' said Cazza.

'Seriously?' Joe said, looking cautious.

Joe was frequently the subject of wind-ups which he was rubbish at spotting, so it was a fair comment.

'Straight up,' I promised, and stretched out my arms to show Joe just how straight up I was. 'It was amazing. I felt like we'd all been transported to some magic land where impossible things happen, like flying trains and talking mice.'

'She's going to be a major star for Wild World if she keeps it up,' Tori said. 'People will come from *miles* to see her. Matt says any extra money Ivana makes for

Wild World can go straight into the rescued-animals side of the park that Mum's developing.'

'You changed your tune about wild animals in circuses, then?' said Cazza.

Tori shook her head vigorously, ignoring the snort coming from Heather Cashman's direction. 'No way! But like they say, each case is different. Ivana's clearly crazy about riding a bike. And if she's OK with it, so am I.'

'And so are her babies,' I said happily. 'Mum hopes they'll be able to reintroduce Boris soon, if what's happening with Anna and Sasha is anything to go by.'

'A bear riding a bike!' Biro was practically choking with laughter. 'Crazy!'

'You'll have to come and watch it for yourselves,' I said.

'Tonight?' said Biro at once.

'Tonight!' Joe squealed.

'Tonight's maybe cool,' said Cazza in a casual kind of voice.

I gloried in the feeling of popularity sizzling about me and my twin sister today. Tori gave me a rather surprising wink.

'Fix it with your folks and it's a date,' I promised, grinning.

13

Black Liquorice Coils

Biro got the day off school on Friday for his moment of fame in Pavlov Valkyrie's film. My school chair felt hot as a boiling brick all day as I wriggled and moaned and watched the classroom clock like a tennis-ball-eating hawk at Wimbledon.

'It's *so* unfair,' I complained as Mum drove us to Harting Park to catch what was left of the filming. She'd borrowed Dr Nik's car, which was a bit clunky but basically had four wheels and enough seats for us all. There was no one at Wild World with the time to babysit Boris, so the young bear sat in a cage strapped securely to the front passenger seat. The bandage was off his leg, although he was still a bit lame. 'Biro missed double maths. *Double*. Can't

Dad get a part in the film for us too?'

'Are you Kurdish? Can you ride a horse bareback and stop with a click of your fingers?' Mum asked.

'No,' I admitted after a pause.

'But she's quite good at handstands,' said Joe loyally.

Joe had been especially keen to come and watch Biro in action on the film set, and had badgered Dad most of yesterday afternoon at what – if the crowds of giggling spectators were anything to go by – was fast becoming known as Ivana's World. Normally Joe's badgering can get quite annoying, but Tori and I were just enjoying the fact that Dad seemed to be hanging around Wild World and Mum a lot more these days, and let it wash over us like a tidal wave of lovely double cream.

'Won't your father miss you?' Dad had said in despair after Joe had presented him with his hundred-and-tenth reason for coming to watch the filming. In the background Ivana pedalled round and round, as calm as an old lady on her daily trip to the shops. 'Here today, Harting Park tomorrow?'

'No,' said Joe. With no mum, and a dad who worked practically twenty-four hours a day, the only things likely to miss Joe were his Warhammer figures.

Cazza had also been keen, but her violin lesson

meant she had to stay in school. 'Totally not bothered,' she'd snarled, after a long row with her mum on her neat little black mobile. 'Never liked horses anyway. Their teeth freak me out.'

'Look!' Joe shouted now as Mum swung up the Harting Park drive. 'The Big Top!'

A massive beige-coloured tent billowed in a field off to the right of the house. It was like something out of a picture book, covered with fluttering pennants and bright bunting. Film trucks were parked around it in a semi-circle. Plainly the circus bit of *The Rose and the Ring* was at the centre of everyone's world today.

Boris started complaining as Mum got out of the car.

'Don't worry, youngster,' she said, opening the baby bear's travelling cage. 'I am not leaving you behind.'

Boris shinned up Mum like she was a pine tree in some wild Russian forest. He was looking like the world's biggest teddy bear now, and was starting to test his sore leg by limping around the kitchen floor and trying to climb on the kitchen chairs.

'Do you think Boris needs a lead, Mum?' I asked as we all made our way over the tussocks in the Big Top field towards the action. 'In case he runs off and gets lost?'

'Not yet, but soon,' Mum said, patting the bear fondly.

'It's not Boris who needs a lead,' Tori said. 'It's Joe. There's a danger we're going to lose him altogether if we don't keep an eye on him.'

Joe was plunging across the field towards the Big Top, his book bag bouncing on his back as he skipped nimbly over the black liquorice coils of electricity cabling that littered the grassy ground. We followed at a gentler pace.

The ring inside the tent was spacious and brightly lit with a combination of old Victorian gas lamps and blazing modern camera lights. The filming equipment took up half the space, and the ring had been arranged so the eye was tricked into thinking it went the whole way around instead of stopping halfway to accommodate the cameras. Gorgeous details were everywhere: old-fashioned baskets full of flowers decorating the ends of the aisles, extras in an amazing selection of feathered hats and thick Victorian coats crammed along the benches as the circus audience, and adverts on the tent walls for things with names like Elliot's Embrocation and Pear's Soap. I saw a dress that I totally wanted, right on the front row near where we were standing, being worn by a girl about my age. How come *she* was in a film wearing pink velvet, and I'd had to spend my day slogging through algebra at Forrests?

We spotted Biro standing with his cousins in the corner of the sawdust ring. They were with a tall man with a strong face and a laugh that boomed around the tent like a cannon. Judging from the puffed-out way the cousins were all standing and the admiring looks on their faces, it had to be the famous Kurdish actor Mirza Khan.

'Biro really looks the part, doesn't he?' said Tori.

Biro looked ace in a billowing white shirt and red neckerchief, dirt on his cheeks and a liveliness about his eyes that told us all what a brilliant day he'd been having. He'd always looked like a horse, but today there was something of a horse's spirit about him too.

The set vet was checking over the actual horses under Uncle Ardalan's beady eye. Film sets took no chances where the welfare of the animals were concerned. The relaxed atmosphere and the way all the Victorian extras sat tapping things on their mobile phones made it clear that everyone was on a break. I saw that the girl in pink velvet had taken out a book with a shiny blue cover that we were studying at school and had buried her nose in it.

'Hi,' I said, seizing my chance to talk to a proper film actor. 'Difficult book, that.'

She looked up at me and smiled. 'You think so? I've got to study it and write an essay on it later.'

'I'm studying it too!' I said in surprise. 'We've got an essay about it next week. So you have to do school work here then, do you?'

The girl laughed. Her shiny old-style brown ringlets – which were *totally* fantastic – bounced like springs on her shoulders. 'Three hours of school every day on set, out in one of the trailers,' she said. 'It was algebra this morning.'

This made me feel much better. 'I'm Taya,' I said. 'My dad organized the horses and one of our friends is doing the riding.'

'Awesome,' said the girl. The modern word didn't really fit with the pink bows in her ringletty hair. 'I'm Ellie.'

'Have you got an important part in the film?' I asked.

'No,' said Ellie honestly. 'I'm playing the main female character Rose de Lacey's younger sister. Basically I don't say much and sit around in pretty dresses.'

'*Seriously* awesome,' I said with feeling.

Biro detached himself from his cousins and came over in our direction.

'That's my friend,' I told Ellie, feeling proud.

'Cute,' said Ellie. Which was weird, because Biro was just Biro.

'Have we missed your bit, Biro?' asked Joe breathlessly.

'Mr Wild is talking with Mr Valkyrie.' Biro suddenly looked quite shy to see us all looking at him. 'My uncle says there are some parts in the script that are not right for Kurdish horse-riding so they are changing them.'

'Mr Valkyrie will love that,' said Tori.

Dad jogged across the ring to join us, his feet sending up little puffs of sawdust. Mum blushed in a pleasing way as he approached. Then the set vet gave a brisk nod confirming that the horses were fit to continue, and everyone moved into position to await instructions – including Biro, who dashed back to his horse. Ellie put her book away as I moved rather hurriedly out of the line of the camera lenses.

'Take two!' Eagle Nose shouted. 'In position. Ride horses around, lot of dust under feet, lot of cheering. Yes?'

'Wouldn't there have been music?' I whispered at Dad as the horses cantered around, their tails swishing as the crowd cheered and stamped and clapped to order. Everything sounded echoey, strange and unfilm-like. Boris lifted his head from Mum's neck and gazed at the scene in blank amazement. A couple of extras slid their gaze towards him, but very professionally slid them back again almost straight away.

'They add the sound at the end,' Tori said knowledgeably. 'You'll hardly recognize this scene when it hits the big screen.'

'OK!' Pavlov Valkyrie shouted after about five takes. 'Good! Thank you! Just two more scenes with horses, no extras.'

The benches of extras all stood up and stretched and took off their hats and scratched their heads and did all those things you do when you've been stuck in one place for ages. Ellie stood up as well, smoothing down the pink velvet dress where it had got crushed into wrinkles. I eyed the dress enviously. It looked just the right size for me.

'What have you got to do now?' I asked, disappointed that she was leaving.

'I'm shooting a scene by the fireplace in the house,' she said. 'It happens straight after the moment Rose confesses that she's in love with Goran, the circus horseman. Kara Montaigne – that's the lady playing our mother, Lady Tempest – gets to throw a fantastic strop. Do you want to come and watch?'

'Oh my wombats,' I said, feeling flustered by this sudden unlooked-for opportunity to watch more filming. 'Totally and completely. Are you sure it'll be OK?'

'Can I come too?' said Joe, looming over my shoulder like a big-eared bat.

'Ellie – Joe; Joe – Ellie,' I said, waving vaguely like I got to introduce film stars to my mates every day of the week. Ellie grinned and Joe blushed.

'Meet us back by the car in half an hour,' said Mum, shifting Boris to her other arm; he weighed a ton. 'Tori, you want to join them?'

'I'm happy here,' said my twin, her eyes trained on her ancient directing hero.

So that's how Joe Morton and I walked right into a tidal wave. Funny how things happen, isn't it?

14

Here You Were and There She Was and Bang!

One of Mr Valkyrie's assistant directors was in charge of Ellie's scene inside the house. Her name was Florence, and she was fluffy from head to toe – from the angel curls on her head to the mohair jumper she wore to the tips of her shaggy-fringed boots.

'Right, Ellie love!' she said cheerily. 'Fireplace scene. Mr Valkyrie's given us a very clear set of instructions how he'd like this played – plenty of fire and fury from your sister and mother while you watch all wide-eyed and still with your needle passing back and forth through your tapestry. It's all about contrasts here. Mr Valkyrie'll be over to check what we've got a bit later. Ready?' She clicked her fingers. 'Make-up needs a little touch-up, Antonio.'

A skinny man with a black ponytail and an armful of exciting cosmetics wove through the cameras and lights towards us. Ellie was pushed into a hard little chair off-camera and powdered vigorously. A wardrobe lady darted in to tweak Ellie's costume and brush away dust from the folds in her skirt.

'Better,' said Florence eventually. She eyed us.

'Friends of mine,' said Ellie. 'You don't mind if they watch, do you?'

'Provided they're quiet,' said Florence in a hard sort of voice. She wasn't half as fluffy as she looked. 'Over there.'

We sat down in the chairs she indicated. Settling his book bag on his lap, Joe kept up a running commentary on everything we were looking at in case I hadn't clocked it for myself.

'I can feel the heat from the fire even over here, or do you think that's the lights? These lights give off more heat than a bonfire, don't they? The firescreen's wicked. Can you see the dragon pattern in the iron? I love dragons. Do you think the marble on the fire surround's real? I didn't know marble came in pink.'

I tore my eyes from the soft folds of Ellie's dress and glimpsed a girl aged about twenty, pacing back and forth beyond the double doors to Harting Park's black-and-white hall. Her dress was a beautiful lemony colour, which made her blonde hair look almost golden. I guessed I was looking at Rose de Lacey, the romantic heroine.

Ellie sat down by the dragon firescreen as directed. A props guy thrust a tapestry of birds on a wooden frame into her hand. The dress spilled off the edge of the sofa like a pink waterfall.

'Ready for a take, Polly?' called Florence.

The girl in lemon gave a smiling thumbs-up through the door.

'Have we got Lady Tempest as well?'

There was an answering shout somewhere behind the lemon-dressed girl.

'Right. And . . . action.'

I sat forward, enthralled as Rose de Lacey – so calm and pretty and lemon-coloured just seconds ago – stormed into the room, her skirts billowing in her wake. An older woman in dark green rustled after her, white-blond hair piled up on her head in the most amazing riot of curls and pins. I recognized her as the lady who'd been smoking a cigarette and having her hem fixed on our first visit to the set. Ellie sewed obediently beside the fire.

'You can't tell me what to do, Mother! I'm of age. I love him!'

'But this is absurd—'

'*You* are absurd. Standing there so cold and remote. You've never felt a moment of passion in your life.'

I watched with delight as the woman playing Lady Tempest swelled, working herself into the strop that Ellie had promised. 'Passion will see you cast out of society, Rose. Passion will lead you to poverty and ruination. You think—'

Joe's book bag slid off his lap and landed with a bang on the floor. Everyone jumped. Lady Tempest faltered and ground to a halt.

'Cut!' shouted Florence. She turned around furiously. 'What the—'

Joe's face was deathly pale apart from two spots of blazing red in the middle of his cheeks, but his voice was as steady as a four-legged chair.

'Hello, Mum.'

Lady Tempest gave a shriek of shock and clapped her hand to her mouth. Polly/Rose de Lacey and Florence the assistant director both gaped. Ellie stabbed herself in the finger with her needle, causing the wardrobe lady to wince and the props guy to rush in and remove the tapestry before it got covered in blood.

'It *is* you, isn't it?' Joe said, like the rest of us weren't there and it was just him and Lady Tempest in the room. 'I know I haven't seen you for a bit and the last time we met your hair wasn't like that, but it's you.'

Lady Tempest lowered her hand. The flashy costume rings she was wearing glinted in the lights. 'Hello, Joe baby,' she said and burst into tears.

Needless to say, the scene was postponed for a few minutes. Crew members hung around, not wanting to get in the way but clearly unable to leave a scene far more gripping than anything Pavlov Valkyrie had dreamed up.

'Don't cry, Mum,' said Joe, patting Lady Tempest's hand as she sobbed on and on. 'It's OK.'

Apart from the red spots on his cheeks, Joe was handling the whole thing magnificently. I wished Lady Tempest – Kara Montaigne... Mrs Morton... or whoever – would stop crying.

'I had an *opportunity*, baby,' said Mrs Morton in a broken sort of voice. 'You know I always wanted to act? Well, I met this man in London who was casting for a film in Hollywood. I mean, *Hollywood*!'

'Yes,' said Joe. 'I've heard of it.'

'Opportunities like that don't come along very often,

especially to ladies who reach a certain age.' Mrs Morton wiped her eyes. 'There was no time – I couldn't come home . . . Your father would never have understood. You understand though, baby, don't you?'

Joe nodded in a stoic sort of way.

'It was hard at first, but I'm getting somewhere at last. This is a big part, Joe baby. Who'd have thought it? Little Kara Montaigne – I changed my name from Karen Morton, so *ageing* – from Fernleigh, playing Lady Tempest for Pavlov Valkyrie!' She stopped crying for long enough to look quite proud of herself.

On cue, Mr Valkyrie himself came striding into the room. The crew – lights, cameras, make-up, props, wardrobe, sound, random people in black polonecks – cringed backwards. Florence the not-so-fluffy director quivered, making the wafty bits on her mohair jumper tremble.

'You have finished scene?' the old eagle demanded.

Mrs Morton pulled her hand from Joe's grasp. 'Pavlov, darling,' she said brightly. 'I've just had the most marvellous reunion with my dear little boy, Joe, here. Such a surprise! We haven't seen each other in a while so we've had a *teensy* delay. I'll be ready for another take in five, Florence.'

She patted Joe tenderly on the cheek, like he was the

one who'd been blubbing his eyes out during their grand reunion. 'We'll have a proper catch-up later on, baby. But now the show must go on!'

She walked away from us without looking back, surrounded by people armed with powder puffs and hairbrushes.

'That was my mum,' said Joe after a minute. 'In case you were wondering.'

'Your mum's an *actress*!' I breathed, reeling from the shock of what I'd just witnessed. 'In *this* film! And you didn't know and here you were and there she was and bang! How weird is that?'

'Pretty weird,' Joe agreed, swallowing.

I goggled at Lady Tempest, sitting with her eyes closed on a chair as Antonio the make-up guy repaired the tear-streaks on her cheeks with a selection of different brushes. I could see her resemblance to Joe now, though I had to squint a bit to imagine her without the Victorian outfit and hair.

'She looks beautiful, doesn't she?' said Joe.

'She looks *amazing*,' I said fervently.

As if all this wasn't enough, there was a sudden crash and a wail of pain. Everyone who wasn't fussing around Lady Tempest dashed towards the fireplace. Ellie was sitting on the floor with her hand held over her eye, looking dazed. People talked urgently, waving plasters and antiseptic cream around. The dragon firescreen lay on its side.

Pavlov Valkyrie strode over to see the damage for himself. He winced and sucked in his skinny cheeks as Ellie gazed up tragically at him with a massive, puffy black eye, complete with blood dribbling from her nose. The wardrobe lady looked like she was going to have a fit at the sight of yet more blood within range of Ellie's precious frock.

'I fell against the firescreen,' Ellie said faintly. 'It hurts.'

And then she leaned forward and threw up on the rug.

15

Major Wombats

More delays.

I decided filming was like riding a bike whose brakes have gone weird. You judder along, thinking you're prepared to put your feet down the next time the brakes decide to kick in, but you still get flung over the handlebars, graze your face and get concussion. Literally, in this case.

Mrs Morton came over as Ellie was rushed away to see a doctor. She stroked Joe's hair absently, like he was still eight. 'What a nuisance! Now Pavlov will have to find a replacement. The girl can't possibly film the rest of her scene looking like she's gone ten rounds in a boxing ring. She'll be out of action for at least a week and we're supposed to finish here on Tuesday.'

You know how a big moment often comes along without any fuss or fanfare, but you remember it somehow as being full of bright lights, drama and excellent music?

'A replacement?' I said.

Pavlov Valkyrie was with not-so-fluffy Florence, examining the footage they'd taken so far on the little camera screen. Before I could talk myself out of what I was about to do, I walked across the room and waited for him to notice me.

'Yes?' he barked at last.

'If you need a replacement for Ellie I'd like to be it,' I blurted. 'I'm quite good at sitting around wearing pretty dresses – well, I would be if I had any, but the only one I owned got burned in a house fire we had, and anyway it was a bit small because Mum bought it when I was a bridesmaid for my aunt Dorina's wedding when I was nine.' I paused for breath before adding a little randomly, 'It was pink.'

Not-so fluffy Florence and Old Eagle Nose looked at me.

'She's right height,' said the director thoughtfully.

'Right age too,' agreed the assistant director.

'Hair is long. Is good.'

'The costume wouldn't need much adjusting. It's the

sister's last scene, so if we're clever with the camera angle we wouldn't need to reshoot anything else.'

I felt the way a cow probably feels when there's farmers standing around discussing how much they're worth.

'No time now, so screen test Tuesday four o'clock,' Pavlov Valkyrie snapped out at me. 'If OK we shoot. If not OK we cut character. Your mother must call and talk to me, fix everything, yes?'

I floated back to Joe and his mum like my shoes were made out of clouds. *I think I just got a part in the film.* We were talking *major* wombats here!

When I reached them, practically exploding with my news, Mrs Morton was in full flow. Joe stood silently beside her.

'—terribly busy tomorrow, baby. I'm going to New York. New York! Imagine!'

It looked like Joe was doing his best to imagine it.

'Then all day Monday I have screen tests for a film back in Hollywood, then back in dear old Fernleigh on Tuesday. The jetleg will be unbearable, but that's the price of fame! Your old mum is turning into quite a globetrotter, isn't she?'

'You're not old,' said Joe.

Mrs Morton turned pink with pleasure. 'Of course

I'm not, baby. I feel twenty-one! So we'll have dinner on Tuesday and have a proper catch-up. You must tell me all about how well you're doing at school and how proud you're making me.'

Pavlov Valkyrie clicked his fingers. 'Kara! Dressing-room scene. Wardrobe needs you for costume change. Florence, all yours. I will take break now.'

As Pavlov Valkyrie left the house and not-so-fluffy Florence resumed charge, Mrs Morton gave Joe a very loud kiss that didn't seem to touch him in any way whatsoever. 'Tuesday, baby,' she said. 'It'll be such a treat!'

She rustled across the floor, away from him.

'See you then, Mum,' Joe said to her back.

I was a bit surprised. It was Friday today, and I'd already worked out that it was four whole days until Tuesday and my screen test. And if that felt like for ever to me . . . well. Let's just say that after three years of nothing, didn't Joe's mum think she ought to crack on with making it up to her son a smidgeon quicker?

The film crew were packing up cameras and taking down lights around the fireplace, heading I supposed for the dressing-room and Mrs Morton's next scene. Joe made a proper effort to stop staring at his mother's dark-green satin back as it disappeared out of the room.

He adjusted his book bag so it hung perfectly straight on his shoulders.

'You've gone a funny pink colour, Taya,' he said, looking at me. 'Like you do when you're all excited. Did something just happen?'

His face was dead pale. I mean, more dead pale than normal. My news suddenly didn't seem very important.

'Nothing interesting,' I said. I linked arms with him. 'Let's go and tell Tori and Biro and Mum and Dad about your mother. They're going to go *nuts*.'

Joe's cheeks had a bit more colour in them by the time we'd trudged back through the house and outside into the February chill.

'You won't believe who we just met,' I said dramatically when we joined the others by Dad's black van. Dad was giving Boris a cuddle and trying to avoid his brand-new nippy little teeth.

'The tooth fairy,' said Tori.

I glanced at Joe in case he wanted to tell everyone. He was staring at the tips of his trainers.

'Kara Montaigne,' I said. 'The actress playing Lady Tempest.'

Blank faces.

'Otherwise known as Karen Morton,' I went on,

enjoying the moment.

'Joe!' Mum gasped. Her hands flew to her throat. 'Your *mother*?'

Joe nodded.

'But how exciting!' Mum practically started weeping as she flung her arms around Joe's neck. She's well emotional about things like this. 'She must have been so happy to see you!'

'I guess,' said Joe, trying to extricate himself from Mum's octopus arms. It took several goes.

'His mum went away to be an *actress*?' Tori whispered to me in astonishment.

'Honestly, Tor, it was like a scene out of a film,' I whispered back. 'I mean, it literally *was* a scene out of a film.'

'Is it OK to give me a lift home, Mr Wild?' Joe sounded very calm. 'I mean, if you're ready to go now?'

'Don't you want to stay until your mother's finished filming so you can catch up a little?' Dad asked. 'She could give you a lift home afterwards.'

'She's going to be busy until late and then she's going away,' Joe said. 'Her last day on the set is Tuesday and we're going to talk then. So if you don't mind giving me a lift back home now, I think I'll do that.'

He got quietly into the back of the black van, settled

his book bag on the seat next to him and buckled himself in.

'Right,' said Dad, looking at a bit of a loss. Joe stared straight ahead, his face practically luminous against the van's dark upholstery. 'Well, Biro and his family are loading up the horses and preparing to take them home to Godalming after a very successful day, so I guess I'm all done here until next week.'

He handed Boris to Mum and the young bear gave a little shout. A few people nearby turned their heads at the unfamiliar sound – and within moments we were surrounded. I guess bear cubs often have that effect.

'He's adorable!'

'I saw you holding him when we were shooting the circus scene, but I thought I was seeing things. Is he yours?'

Boris was properly awake now and looked interested at the faces cooing around him. He gave a sneeze and seemed to wipe his nose with a fluffy paw. Then . . .

'Someone says there is bear here.'

The gawkers slid away as Pavlov Valkyrie appeared from a long dark trailer parked a few metres from Dad's van. In the light spilling from the trailer's open door, the director gazed at Boris. Beside me I could feel Tori holding her breath at being this close to her hero.

'You bring me this bear for my film,' he said to Dad, like he was stating a fact.

'Well,' Dad began.

'Original script for film had bears,' said the director. 'Circus have bears when I was boy.'

'Yes, but—' said Dad.

'I did not find bears so we cut. You find bears. I will use you for many more films, I think.'

'That's very nice of you, Mr Valkyrie, but—' said Dad.

Pavlov Valkyrie didn't look as if he was listening. 'We will include little bear in final circus scenes we are shooting on Tuesday.'

'*Mr* Valkyrie,' said Mum.

The way she said 'Mr' made the old director jump a bit.

'I am sorry, but this bear is not available for your film.' Mum tickled Boris gently behind the ears and prepared to put him into the cage still strapped to the front seat of Dr Nik's car. 'He's too young. And it's time for his tea.'

16

Magic Pigeon

Tori was laughing in the darkness of our bedroom. We were supposed to be asleep but, after the day we'd had, it was proving tricky to switch our brains off.

'Mr Valkyrie's face when Mum said no . . .' she choked.

I propped myself up on my elbow. 'He's too young,' I said in Mum's chocolatey accent. 'And it's time for his tea.'

Tori laughed a bit more. 'I don't think anyone ever says no when Mr Valkyrie asks for something.'

'I thought you liked him?'

'I like his *work*,' Tori said. 'But *he's* a nightmare. He was really bossy on the film set today. You missed most of it when you went into the house with Joe and that girl you were talking to but, believe me, if I'd been one of his actors I would have quit for sure.'

The fluttery feeling I'd had ever since Mr Valkyrie had told me I could do a screen test on Tuesday came back to bomb gleefully around in my tummy like a supercharged butterfly. I still hadn't told Tori about it – somehow I knew she'd take the mickey – though I'd managed a quiet word with Mum about phoning up Mr Valkyrie and giving permission and not telling Tori. Mum had been so cool about it – compared to her fiery reaction on the subject of Boris – that part of me wondered if she'd actually heard what I said.

'Perhaps we should tell Mr Valkyrie about Ivana,' I said.

'I will have big bear in my film.' Tori made her voice deep and fierce. 'With bicycle. Yes?'

We started laughing again.

'I hope Joe's all right,' said Tori as we calmed down. 'And his dad.'

'It must be the weirdest thing ever, having your mum or your wife disappear and reappear on you like some kind of magic pigeon,' I said, trying to imagine it. '*Pouf!* She's gone. *Pouf!* She's back.'

'Magic pigeon?' Tori repeated. 'You really know how

to express an emotional trauma like this, don't you, Taya?'

'What did you do, eat a dictionary?' I demanded.

I went into a silent huff for a bit, but there was still lots to talk about so it didn't last long.

'Mum and Dad were looking pretty cosy today,' I said eventually. 'I reckon Dad'll be back home with us next week.'

'That would be . . . good.'

'In other words you're flying around on a little brain trapeze of happiness at the thought,' I said helpfully. My sister sometimes has trouble expressing big emotions, so I'm always there to help her along.

'When do you think Mum and Dr Nik will try and put Boris back in with Ivana?' Tori asked in a very unobvious attempt to change the subject.

'It's next week or never, Mum said.'

Tori sounded shocked. '*Never?*'

'I know,' I agreed. 'I was shocked too. Apparently it's well difficult to reintroduce bear cubs to their mothers, and it gets harder the longer you leave it.'

I didn't want to lose Boris, but at the same time I knew the best place for him was with his mother and sisters. If Ivana rejected him . . . Well, it wasn't something I wanted to think about much.

I snuggled down, listening to the grunts and howls of the Wild World animals outside the window. I hoped I would get to be in the film. I hoped Mrs Morton was thinking about Joe. I hoped Dad was thinking about Mum. I hoped that before long Boris would be back with his own family. I hoped lots of things.

'Night, then,' said my sister.

'Night,' I yawned back.

'Dad couldn't believe it when I told him. He said some pretty rude things about the way she left us without any explanations and how she had always been pretty selfish, but I don't think he meant it in a nasty way.'

It was Monday morning in our form room and Joe was looking at me expectantly, waiting for a reply.

'What?' I said, pulling myself out of a nice rambling daydream I'd been having about doing my screen test tomorrow and then being discovered and getting dead rich and famous and well dressed.

'I said Dad didn't mean the rude stuff he said about Mum in a nasty way,' Joe repeated.

'How can rude stuff be nice?' Tori asked curiously.

I winced. My sister has a habit of being direct when

sometimes you have to kind of *wiggle* your way around a question.

'My parents, like, truly genuinely hate each other's guts and they're even still married,' said Cazza.

Joe flushed a bit, but recovered his thread. 'Dad was really mad at the time but he can be rude now without meaning it because we're totally over it. I'm totally over it. Totally.'

'Course you are,' I said supportively. Tori was still frowning, but Cazza'd lost interest and had gone back to drawing a skull on the back of her hand which she'd said was a design for the tattoo she was going to get for her next birthday.

'And I actually think it's awesome that Mum's an actress because she did always really want to be one and she's getting famous now,' Joe went on.

'That's brilliant, Joe,' I said. 'Bet you're looking forward to seeing her tomorrow.'

'I can't wait,' Joe said brightly. 'Dad nearly told me I couldn't go back to Harting Park tomorrow to see Mum but I persuaded him that it would be OK. I bet she's done loads of really interesting things. We're going to talk the roof off I expect.'

The bell went and we bundled out of our form room for art. Joe walked a bit ahead, next to Biro.

Biro looked like he was walking taller than normal, as if his film experience on Friday had added a few centimetres to his height. He was doing more filming tomorrow. I wondered with a rush of excitement if doing a scene in a gorgeous Victorian dress would make me look taller too. *If* I got the part, I reminded myself. A screen test didn't automatically mean fame and fortune.

As I walked behind Joe, I noticed that he seemed strangely thin from this angle. At first I thought it was because of the way he contrasted with Biro's new extra tallness until I realized he'd left his book bag in the classroom.

I hurried to catch up with him. 'Don't you want your bag?' I asked in a low voice. I didn't want to have a scene in the middle of the corridor like last time.

'There's no point having Mum's picture in art today when I'm actually going to tell her about everything in person tomorrow,' Joe explained, frowning at me like I'd said something really thick – which, let's face it, isn't unusual.

I pictured Mrs Morton's face squished up in the bottom of Joe's bag in the empty form room, cheek to cheek with his books, a bunch of pens, and most likely an old crisp packet or snotty tissue, if his bag was anything like mine. *Best place for it,* I thought before I could stop myself.

'Guess not,' I said out loud.

17

Small-Satsuma-Light

When we got home, we had a bit of trouble getting in the door.

'Mum!' Tori shouted as we stared in disbelief at our hallway. 'Are you in there?'

You never saw so many flowers in one place in your life. There were lilies and roses and a whole lot of more exotic ones that I'd never seen before, all standing bunched together in the hall and blocking the way to the kitchen, sitting room and stairs. For some crazy reason, our house had turned into a florist's shop.

'Come around the back, *queridas*!' Mum shouted, somewhere off to the left.

'Do you think Dad's done this?' I gasped as we hurried round to the back door. 'Or Dr Nik?'

'If either of them did, it's a stupid waste,' said Tori crossly.

It *was* a bit over the top, even for a romantic gesture. I pictured a whole lot of very disappointed bees as they zoomed to where the flowers had probably been growing right up until today. They probably all wept little bee tears and had to make do with a bunch of uninteresting buttercups in the corner instead of their normal exotic banquet.

Mum was on the phone, pacing up and down the kitchen as we came in the back door. The smell of lilies drifting in from the hallway practically knocked us out. An empty bottle of baby milk lay on its side on the kitchen counter. I looked up to see that Boris had climbed the kitchen curtain and was clinging on at the top like one of those grippy toys you put on the end of your pencil. The curtain pole was bending in an alarming sort of way.

'. . . the young bear in my care is not old enough to be used in your film, Mr Valkyrie, and a whole world full of flowers will not change my mind. This is a working wildlife park and the welfare of the animals is more important than your movie. Goodbye.'

We goggled at Mum as she put the phone back into its cradle with a decisive bang. '*Film directors!*' she said, in the tone of voice usually saved for Rabbit's little parcels on the lawn.

'Pavlov Valkyrie sent you the flowers?' said Tori.

'He thinks he can have anything that he wants,' Mum growled. 'Well, someone who spends hundreds of pounds on flowers – pounds that we could use to help the animals in our care – just to get his own way needs to learn a lesson! I say no and I mean no!'

Boris shouted for help getting down from his position on the curtains. Still growling to herself, Mum hefted him down and put him in Rabbit's basket. Rabbit rushed across the room as fast as her creaky legs would let her and started licking Boris's head with excitement before snuggling up with him.

The air was thick with lily fumes. Tori coughed. 'Can we get rid of the flowers before we all suffocate?' she pleaded.

'They well pong,' I added in agreement.

Mum scratched her head and stared at the flowers clogging up the hall. 'Maybe we can take them to Milstead Hospital,' she said.

'Ellie – the girl who had the accident on sct she's in Milstead Hospital, Mum,' I remembered out loud. 'Can we make sure she gets some?'

'Of course, *querida*,' said Mum. Her eyes gleamed.

'All the more reason to arrange a courier and send the bill to Mr Valkyrie, I think.'

'What accident?' asked Tori.

I was saved from explaining – and fessing up about my screen test – as a pair of snores started wafting out of Rabbit's basket. Boris lay nestled neatly between Rabbit's paws and they were both asleep.

'Look at them,' said Mum fondly. 'They are made for each other.'

'Except Rabbit's a dog and Boris is a bear,' Tori said.

I bent down and stroked Rabbit's ears. She twitched and snuggled closer to Boris. 'Try telling Rabbit that,' I said.

Tuesday dawned with much less of a dazzle than any day of screen tests, movie-making and long-lost mothers ought to have done. I brushed my teeth at least ten times, even though I knew the effect would have worn off by the time we got to Harting Park and I'd probably smell of Wotsits or some other post-school snack instead. I imagined Joe was doing the same thing.

Tori banged on the bathroom door as I practised smiling in the mirror. 'Have you fainted? Or died? We'll miss our bus!'

Tori still didn't know about my screen test. I'd got to the point where it would feel weird telling her now.

'Think positive,' I told my reflection sternly, brushing my hair twenty more times for luck. 'They wouldn't have called you if they didn't think you were a good match for Ellie.'

Even if I got the test, they would only film the back of my head so they could put the scene together with all the stuff Ellie'd already done and avoid a total re-shoot of everything. It wasn't exactly going to be the limelight. I wondered if there was any such thing as the small-satsuma-light-that's-gone-a-bit-soft-in-the-fruitbowl because that was probably what I was going to be in.

Tori banged on the door again. 'HELLO?'

The bus from Wild World takes longer to get to school than the bus did from our old house across Fernleigh Common. But it was a small price to pay for living with the animals. Joe was pacing around the form room when we got there. He was on to us in seconds.

'Is my hair OK? I tried to stop it sticking up at the back in the bathroom this morning but I don't think it worked. Not that Mum will mind what I look like of course, but I kind of mind because I want her to have a good impression. I got a zit on my neck this morning but I think my shirt collar covers it. Does it cover it? Can you see it?'

'No need to show us,' I said hurriedly as he started yanking at his collar and stretching up his chin.

Joe's restlessness lasted all morning. At lunch he was so twitchy that he hardly ate a thing.

'It's PE this afternoon, Joe,' Tori said as I tried to quell my own butterflies and eat the pasta in front of me. 'You're going to pass out in the sports hall if you don't eat and then they'll send you home and you won't be able to get to Harting Park at all.'

'I'm not very hungry,' Joe confessed. He pushed a carrot across his plate to join a pile of other carrots suffering the same uneaten fate.

'She's just your mum,' said Cazza in a bored voice.

'Joe,' Tori said loudly, 'Cazza's got a gob on her like an express train. We all know how important this afternoon is for you.'

'It's all just a dumb fuss about nothing,' Cazza snarled. 'You're like actually well lucky, Joe, because my mum never disappears even though I totally wish she would.'

She grabbed her tray and marched away from our table.

'Cazza's mum confiscated her phone last night,' said Tori by way of explanation. 'Ignore her.'

18

Huff-Huff-Huffing

We successfully did as Tori suggested for the rest of the afternoon. Joe was so twitchy it actually wasn't that hard, because all our energies were concentrated on keeping his feet on the ground. Cazza calmed down again and was exchanging cryptic *Doctor Who* quotes with Tor by the end of the day.

Dad was standing by the van checking his watch when we finally tumbled out of the school gates, ducking and diving among thronging school uniforms like grey seals racing through their colony on a special blubber-fetching mission.

'Quick as you can, I'm not supposed to have left the set,' said Dad, sounding a bit agitated.

Joe was fumbling with his seatbelt so badly that I

reached over and did it for him. And we were off, rolling towards fame, fortune and Joe's missing mum.

Joe was silent for obvious reasons, I was thinking about my screen test, and Tori was in Tori World. So as we drove along, Dad did all the talking. We heard his opinion on the flowers Old Eagle Nose had sent Mum in a bid to get Boris into his film – 'Totally daft, was never going to work' – and about the amazing black eye that the make-up artist had done for Mirza Khan's character, Goran, after Rose de Lacey's dad pushes him over in the mud and wallops him, and how Wardrobe had run out of clean white linen shirts because Mr Valkyrie had made everyone shoot the fight scene – where Goran's shirt starts off clean and ends up covered in mud – too many times.

'And our Kurdish horses have been stars,' said Dad warmly. 'Mr Valkyrie has worked Biro and his family hard but everyone seems happy with the end result. Biro's uncle and Mirza Khan have been getting along so well that they're almost booking holidays together.'

He turned the van in through the Harting Park gates – and I thought I was seeing things. Even Joe and Tori woke up and almost shoved me aside to get their noses to the van window as well.

'Did it *snow* here?' I asked incredulously, taking in the fluffy whiteness that had transformed the front of the big house.

There were icicles along the gutters and dangling down from the lanterns that hung on either side of the front door; deep piles of snow had drifted up against the steps; frost and snow made patterns on the long paned windows. The whole house looked like something off a Christmas card, while everywhere else there was just the normal mud and greyness that comes with a late-February afternoon.

'Snow machine,' Dad explained as he parked beside Biro's uncle's massive horse van. 'They shot some Christmas scenes at the house today. I think your mother's finishing a couple of scenes in the circus tent, Joe. Shall we go and take a look? Let's hope Mr Valkyrie didn't need me for anything while I was gone.'

'He can hardly sack you now, Dad,' said Tori as we left the magical snow scene behind and hurried over the muddy field towards the Big Top. 'He's filmed the horses already.'

We watched Joe striding ahead of Dad towards the circus tent, practically tripping over his big feet in his rush to get there.

'Do you think he's going to be OK?' my sister asked.

'I don't know,' I admitted. 'All I can say is that I hope his mum shows a bit more interest in him than she did on Friday.'

It didn't look like Pavlov Valkyrie had missed Dad at all. When we reached the tent, he was talking earnestly with Uncle Ardalan, one hand resting on the shaggy mane of the nearest Kurdish horse while the set builders tweaked bits of circus tent to make them hang straight. I couldn't see Biro.

'Mum's there,' said Joe suddenly. 'I'll catch her before the next scene.'

Mrs Morton was standing and laughing with the one of the lighting guys as the make-up artist patted her around the chin with a powder puff that reminded me of a rabbit's tail. She looked fantastic in a rustling black gown, her hair coiled up on her head like a nest of fat golden snakes. But our view of the reunion was blocked as Mr Valkyrie loomed up on Dad's right.

'Horses are all finished,' he pronounced, wrapping a long bony arm round Dad's shoulders. 'I shoot one more scene and then we talk about bear.'

Tori and I exchanged glances. Didn't this guy ever give up?

'I send flowers to your wife and I get nothing,' the

director said, sounding put out. 'You will talk to her. You will make your wife understand importance of my film.'

'It's not up to me, Mr Valkyrie,' said Dad.

The director made a sort of *pfut* noise. 'She is your wife. She will listen.'

Dad scratched his beard. 'Believe me, sir, our relationship doesn't work like that.'

'Understatement of the century,' Tori whispered to me.

Mum and Dad were getting on a lot better than they had since Christmas, but it was still a bit of a dance round a boxing ring and we weren't counting eggs, let alone full-grown chickens.

As Uncle Ardalan and two of Biro's cousins led the horses off the set and people scurried about with rakes and dustpans to tidy up the sawdust, a black-shirted minion appeared at Old Eagle Nose's elbow. 'Ready for the next scene, Mr Valkyrie sir.'

'We will talk after,' pronounced the director, before stalking towards a nearby camera. Dad looked resigned.

I suddenly saw Joe rushing towards the tent flaps, looking very tall and stiff with his chin practically pointing at the tent roof the way it does when he's trying not to cry. Instead of following her son, Mrs

Morton was taking up position in the middle of the circus ring and doing some sort of complicated breathing exercise.

'Why do I get the feeling something just went wrong?' asked Tori. It looked like she'd spotted Joe too.

Anger started charging through my belly like a herd of stampeding hippos. 'I know you're not supposed to be rude to grown-ups,' I began furiously, 'but I could *honestly* tell Mrs Morton a few things about—'

Tori ran after Joe's disappearing back, leaving me in mid-rant. After a brief hesitation, I decided maybe Tori would be better at talking to Joe just now. She would be calmer than me.

Mirza Khan appeared on the set, adjusting the neck of his loose white shirt. He nodded at the director. Mrs Morton stopped her little huff-huff-huffing exercise and nodded as well.

'Action!' shouted Mr Valkyrie.

'My daughter was born into a world you will never understand!' cried Lady Tempest. 'If you take her away, she will die of unhappiness. And if you wish to kill her, then you do not love her.'

Joe's mum may have been a lousy mother, but she was a pretty good actor. I hadn't had much of a chance to see her in action as her shouty scene in the house had been cut short – but this was the real thing. As for Mirza Khan, pacing up and down in dusty breeches in front of the stately Lady Tempest in her long black dress, he had a delicious voice that reminded me of a dark chocolate biscuit. The fantastic black eye Dad had told us about was on his handsome face and looked painful. It was hard to remember that it was fake.

'You speak to me as if I could control this, Lady Tempest. Your daughter has a mind of her own. I can no more change her than I can change the direction of the wind.'

'You will change her. You must.'

Lady Tempest glowered at the dusty horseman before sweeping off-camera like a ferocious black crow. Mirza Khan slowly crumpled to his knees with his head in his hands. The whole tent held its breath for what felt like *ages* until Mr Valkyrie shouted: 'Cut!'

Everyone started chattering and peering at the little screens on the back of the cameras. As I breathed out, I felt like someone had sprinkled magic dust in my eyes. I had to blink a couple of times to clear the dancing images.

'That was *awesome*,' I said.

But clearly it wasn't awesome because Mr Valkyrie made them shoot it four more times, making a minion brush the sawdust off Mirza Khan's knees before each take. By the fifth go I was starting to find the scene a bit daft, although the actors attacked the words and did the acting like new each time.

'You speak as if I could control this, Lady Tempest . . .'

'You speak . . .'

'You speak as if . . .'

At last Mr Valkyrie shouted 'Cut!' and seemed happy with what they'd got. The tent breathed a collective sigh of relief. There was a brief pause . . . and Old Eagle Nose was back and clapping Dad round the shoulders again.

'Bear,' he said gently but firmly, in case Dad needed reminding of what he wanted to talk about. 'Your wife is foster carer but manager at wildlife park will make final decision. I will speak to him.'

'It's true that the bear is the ultimate responsibility of the wildlife park, Mr Valkyrie, but I can tell you now that the manager will back my wife one hundred per cent,' said Dad. 'Boris really is too young to work on a film set.'

Mr Valkyrie looked furious. He removed his arm from Dad's shoulders. Visions of all the work the old director might be able to bring Dad – or stop Dad from getting – came floating into my head.

'What about Ivana, Dad?' I blurted. 'She's older and we know she likes performing.'

'What is Ivana?' Pavlov Valkyrie rapped out.

'She used to belong to a circus in Russia and was ignoring her cubs – that's why Mum had to foster the little one, Boris – but we worked out that she was missing this trick she used to do in the circus,' I explained.

Mr Valkyrie looked at me intently. 'What is trick?'

'Riding a bike,' I said. 'It's totally hilarious because it makes her so happy. She's all gentle and lovely with her cubs these days. We're going to reintroduce Boris to her soon, with any luck.'

'I want big bear,' said Mr Valkyrie at once. 'I will have bear on bicycle for my film.'

He sounded so like Tori's impression of him the other night that I got this awful fit of the giggles. As Dad made furious faces at me, Mr Valkyrie's bushy eyebrows practically shot off his head.

I had to hold my sides. 'I'm sorry,' I gasped. 'It's just . . . my sister . . .' And I was off again. It was quite embarrassing actually, but there was nothing I could do but ride the giggle wave.

The director turned his attention back to Dad as I

heaved and gulped and sobbed and roared myself more stupid than normal. 'I want to see big bear now and discuss with manager. Is wildlife park far?'

Looking defeated, Dad checked his watch. 'It's a fifteen-minute drive from here, so we could be there by four-thirty. Do you have the time?'

'I will make time,' said the director. 'I will call my driver.'

I stopped laughing abruptly as the giggle wave smashed good and hard into the shore of a real live disaster. If four-thirty was in fifteen minutes' time . . .

I was late for my screen test!

19

Approximately Ten Thousand Kittens

'Oh wombats, wombats, wombats,' I moaned, rushing across the muddy field. How could I have forgotten the most important appointment of *my whole life*? I was a ditz of major ditz proportions. They would pickle my brain for scientific study in years to come. 'Gather round, ladies and gentlemen, and share my amazement at this peculiar specimen. Somehow the owner of this brain managed to function in her daily life with the crucial remembering-stuff lobe entirely missing.'

I stopped in the car park, panting loudly, and checked my watch. Nearly twenty past four already. It was like one of those dreams when you're supposed to be somewhere and time is just running away like water.

Where was I supposed to go? I guessed back in the house, where they'd been shooting the original scene. Head down, I charged for the front door like a mad-eyed, mildly freckled bull.

People seemed to be putting away their equipment with that air of 'job done, need a cup of tea' that Mum gets when she's fed her babies and they're snoozing in Rabbit's basket. The freestanding camera lights were being folded up and disconnected. My heart, which was already somewhere around my knees, now sank right down to my toes.

'Excuse me,' I gasped at a nearby clapperboard person. 'Did I miss the screen test?'

She looked at me in surprise. 'Florence has everything she needs. No need to do it again.'

'But I haven't done it yet,' I said.

'Course you have, love,' said Clapperboard, in the slow and patient voice teachers sometimes use with me when I'm taking my time grasping an idea. 'Talk it through with Florence if you like. She's over there with . . .' Looking over my shoulder, she faltered. 'Um. I was going to say . . . you?'

I whirled round. Tori stood by the not-so-fluffy Florence, wearing a look of thunder, a set of amazing brown ringlets – and the pink velvet dress.

My pink velvet dress.

Florence blinked as I marched up and jabbed my sister in the chest.

'*What are you doing?*' I hissed.

'You think I *want* to look like a pink blancmange with curly spaniel ears?' Tori was tight-faced with fury. 'I was running in here after Joe when they grabbed me, stuck a camera in my face, tortured my hair with hot tongs, shoved me into this thing and *finally* put me by the fireplace with some sewing in my hand. *Sewing!* And no one would listen when I said I'd only come in here to find my friend!'

'B . . . b . . . but . . .' said Florence weakly.

I was beside myself. 'This was my big chance and you took it from me! You don't *want* to be an actor! *You don't even like the dress!*' Which quite frankly was the most infuriating bit of this whole disaster.

'But . . .' Florence bleated again.

The people in the room had noticed the two of us and started pointing and laughing in a startled sort of way.

'I had no choice!' Tori roared back. Her ringlets bobbed weirdly at me. 'Didn't you hear me? No one was listening when I said I didn't want to do it. I don't know where poor Joe is and I hate this dress and my stupid hair makes me want to die of shame and I'm so totally furious right now that I feel like *exploding*!'

'There's two of you,' said Florence.

We both snapped our heads round and glared at her.

'So?' we both snarled at the same time.

Florence's mohair jumper trembled. 'Was it *you* that was supposed to do the part?' she asked me helplessly.

'Yes!' I wailed.

Tori's eyes narrowed. 'You *knew* about this? How come *I* didn't?'

'I didn't tell you, OK? I just forgot. Well,' I amended, still fizzing, 'I didn't forget exactly, but I knew you'd take the mickey so I just left it out of our conversations, all right?'

Tori advanced on me. 'My hair *bounces*,' she said. 'Do you have any idea how that feels?'

'OK, I see what's happened here,' Florence said, trying to sound soothing. 'I'm sorry, but we're striking the set now and we won't be reshooting – we have what we need. Time to get you out of that dress, young lady, and send you home. Thank you for your time . . .'

I was snorting like an asthmatic buffalo. *It was so unfair.*

'I HATE YOU AND I WISH YOU WEREN'T MY SISTER!' I shrieked.

'I HATE YOU TOO!' Tori shrieked back.

Bang on cue, Dad came jogging into the house. 'Tori! Taya! There you are. Any idea where Joe is? Mr Valkyrie wants to go to Wild World and he doesn't have much time and his driver is waiting . . .'

He trailed off. Tori and I were yelling at each other like banshees on a bad day, practically ripping hunks of hair out of each other's heads. Florence was trying her best to separate us and avoid our flying fists while the wardrobe lady moaned and wrung her hands on the sidelines, shouting helpful stuff like: 'Don't rip the bodice! Take care of the lace on the sleeves!'

Dad strode over and grabbed me round the waist, dragging me back. Tori raced out of the room, followed by the wardrobe lady who looked like she was having approximately ten thousand kittens.

'Put me down, Dad,' I sobbed, whirling my arms and kicking my legs helplessly in the air. 'Tori's such a cow.'

Dad marched out of the house and dumped me in a large pile of snow-machine snow outside the door – which, let me tell you, was just as cold and wet as if it had fallen from the sky.

'You are a *disgrace*,' Dad roared as I gasped and floundered around. 'I hope I never see you brawling in public like that again. This is the last time I bring you to a film set. Ever.'

I burst into tears as Dad went back into the house. 'I hope you throw Tori in here too because she totally started this!' I squealed after him.

Mr Valkyrie came walking towards me from the direction of a shiny black car, holding out a bony hand. I blinked at his fingers through swimming tears a couple of times until I realized he was offering to pull me out of the snowdrift.

'And I was thinking English people are not passionate,' he said, looking amused as I let him heave me out.

'My mother is Portuguese,' I sniffed, and Mr Valkyrie nodded as if that explained a lot.

'Tell your father I wait in car with my driver,' he said, before heading back to the shiny black car and getting in the back seat.

Tori came out with Dad. She was back in school uniform and the pink velvet dress was gone – most likely rushed to some kind of dress hospital for resuscitation. My twin had scraped her ringlets back into her normal rubber band and was gazing firmly at her feet.

'Apologize to your sister, Taya,' Dad ordered. Steam

still looked like it was coming out of his ears. 'And then I want you to go back in there and apologize to every single member of Mr Valkyrie's team.'

I almost fell into the drift again. '*Me* apologize to *her*?' I said, aghast. I flashed a look at Tori, who was still staring at the ground. 'And then . . . and then to everyone else?'

Dad folded his arms. 'If you don't, I will tell your mother, and that little dump in the snow will be like a paddle on a Mediterranean beach.'

I gulped. If Mum heard about this, she would go completely and utterly *nutsville* and I'd have to leave home and go and live in the ape house with Honey and Grandpa. Slowly, I straightened my school jacket.

'Sorry,' I said sulkily, refusing to look at my sister. Then, before Dad could grab me and make me say it again 'and mean it this time', I went into the house to find all the other people to apologize to. It wasn't exactly how I'd planned to spend my afternoon.

'Sorry . . . Sorry . . . I'm really sorry . . .'

I was starting to get a sense of what Mrs Morton and Mirza Khan must have felt like doing their scene over and over again by the time I reached the fifth smirking/disapproving person to apologize to.

'Sorry . . . I'm really honestly sorry . . .'

The more I said it, the more I found I was squirming about what I'd done. I went from room to room.

'Sorry . . . Sorry . . . Sorry— Joe?'

Joe blinked up at me with red eyes from a dark corner tucked just underneath the big sweeping Harting Park stairs. 'Oh,' he said. 'Hi, Taya. Sorry for what?'

20

Quantity of Noughts

I was feeling physically hot with embarrassment about what I'd done by this point. 'Actually, Joe, I think the more important question is: are you OK?'

Joe shrugged.

'What did your mum say to you?' I asked cautiously.

'She got a callback from Hollywood inviting her to do the film she auditioned for yesterday,' he said. 'Which is good and everything, but she's going to have to catch a flight at six o'clock tonight back to Los Angeles so she can't have dinner with me like we planned. I got a bit upset.'

I ducked under the stairs and sat next to him. 'Some people . . . are just not very good at the important stuff,' I said at last.

We stayed like that for a bit, side by side in the dark, watching people carrying nameless equipment back and forth through the hall.

'Dad needs to take Mr Valkyrie to Wild World,' I said in the end. 'He wants to talk to Matt about using Ivana in the film. So I think maybe we'd better . . .'

We went back outside. Dad and Mr Valkyrie were talking about something beside the van while the director's driver sat patiently at the wheel of the black car; Tori was sitting in the van's front seat. Standing a little apart was a tall man with messy fair hair and glasses, pacing anxiously beside a big silver car.

'It's Dad,' Joe said, stopping in surprise. 'What's he doing here?'

Mr Morton spotted us and gave a kind of uncoordinated flap of his hand which completely reminded me of Joe.

'He's come to take you home,' I guessed.

Joe started walking slowly towards his dad – and then a bit quicker. They clashed in an uncomfortable-looking Morton-ish hug, all elbows and good intentions, and stayed like that for some time before Mr Morton ruffled Joe's hair with a clumsy tenderness and helped him into the big silver car.

Family was the most important thing in the world, I

thought. I was luckier than I'd ever realized.

I walked over to Dad and kissed him apologetically on the cheek. Then I opened the van door and peered in at my twin.

'Sorry for being such a total and utter doughnut, Tor,' I said.

'You're a whole *tray* of doughnuts,' Tori replied coolly.

'An entire bakery of pastries, all flavours and extremely stale,' I agreed.

'Get in the blinking van, will you?' said Tori.

Even in the freezing darkness of a late-February afternoon, Mr Valkyrie couldn't take his eyes off Ivana and her bicycle. The park was closing so the other spectators were drifting home, but Pavlov Valkyrie stayed exactly where he was, tall and thin in his big woolly overcoat and fake-fur hat like he didn't feel the cold at all. We stood with him patiently, trying not to shiver. Mum was feeding Boris back at home, and had promised to come out and join us as soon as she'd finished. Dr Nik was away, but Matt, reunited with his beloved electric buggy, was sorting out a problem in the tropical house and had also promised to come over as soon as possible.

Ivana stopped pedalling with a grunt and shambled back to the den to feed Anna and Sasha.

'Bicycle wheels will be dangerous for cubs,' Mr Valkyrie commented.

'Bear cubs don't emerge from the den until they are around ten weeks old,' Dad replied. 'These youngsters have two or three more weeks to go until then. I understand that the team's made plans to keep Ivana happy and the cubs safe when the time comes.'

The plans were basically to put a second fenced enclosure inside the first, a sort of cycling track, where Ivana could ride her bike and not squish her family.

Mr Valkyrie's phone rang, but he ignored it. 'My people will arrange old-style bicycle,' he said. 'Old bicycles are different from new bicycles. You will leave it with bear and she can try. If she likes it, we will film her.'

'Mr Valkyrie, we still haven't spoken to the park manager about any of this,' Dad reminded the director patiently.

Like an actor making a perfectly timed entrance, Matt came trundling over the brow of the dark hill on his buggy. He parked under the nearest lamp post and leaped out, striding towards Eagle Nose with his hand extended.

'Mr Valkyrie, it's an honour,' he said, shaking the director's bony fingers. 'I understand you are interested in using Ivana in your film? We may have a problem with that, unfortunately.'

The film director's eyebrows did their beetly thing.

'Ivana's had a lot of unsettling things happening in her life in the last six months – leaving a familiar place and routine, spending time in quarantine, cubbing, and moving here to Wild World,' Matt went on, looking unruffled. 'On top of this, we urgently need to reintroduce the young bear cub I believe you met on your film set the other day: a tricky operation at the best of times. We really cannot move Ivana again.'

'I don't say we must move her,' said the film director.

Matt frowned. 'But I thought you were filming at Harting Park?'

The film director gave a shrug. 'We can film here. And there will be generous fee.'

He named a stupendous sum of money that made my eyes water. I'm no expert, but it sounded like the deal was enough to keep Ivana and her cubs in a bear's version of champagne and chocolate truffles for several lifetimes.

Mum came towards us, muffled up in a trailing scarf and long coat with Boris and Rabbit shambling at her heels on matching leads. Rabbit woofed in a friendly way. Mum handed us the leads and looked Mr Valkyrie up and down disapprovingly.

'Anita,' said Matt, looking like he was still digesting the quantity of noughts in the fee that the film director had offered. 'I understand you've already met Mr Valkyrie?'

The old director took one of Mum's hands and kissed it. Dad looked a little annoyed.

'Mrs Wild, I apologize for inappropriate flowers.'

'I hope the patients at Milstead Hospital enjoyed them,' said Mum beadily. She rested her free hand on Boris's head as the cub sat by my side with his long claws splayed out on the tarmac path. He felt warm and heavy against my leg.

'Yes,' agreed the director, sounding almost humble. 'I received thanks from girl injured on set, which I pass to you.'

'Is she better now?' Tori asked.

I'd explained about Ellie in the van on the way here. Tori still thought I was a doughnut, but hadn't tried to hit me even once. Maybe because I'd told her about Joe as well, and she'd had the same blinding revelation about families as me.

'Yes. She is back at work on new film in Czech

Republic next month,' the director said.

A ripped Victorian dress snuck accusingly into my head even as I trembled with envy at the thought of Ellie's life. I was glad she was OK.

'I understand and accept that your bear is too young for film,' said the director, releasing Mum's fingers. 'Now we negotiate to film big bear here in park instead.'

'If you filmed here, would you have to close the park to the public, Mr Valkyrie?' Tori asked.

'This will be inconvenient but necessary,' said the director. 'So I will increase offer by fifty thousand pounds. You will do many wonderful things for animals with this money, I am sure.'

'We will discuss it and let you know in the morning, Mr Valkyrie,' said Matt coolly, like people offered that kind of money to Wild World every day.

The director seemed to sense that the discussion was over. With a nod, he strode off towards the park gates where his driver was waiting patiently. Only when he was out of sight did Mum whoop and jump into Dad's arms.

21

No Way, Santa Fé

Dad froze with surprise. After a couple of seconds, Mum slithered down again, looking flustered.

'Cup of tea at my place to discuss this?' said Matt loudly. 'Who wants a lift in the buggy?'

I glanced at Tori. If we went in the buggy, Mum and Dad would have to walk the animals over to Matt's. In the dark. Alone – apart from Rabbit and Boris.

'Us,' we both said at once.

Mum took Boris's lead from me and Dad took Rabbit's from Tori. I rubbed Boris on the shaggy fur between his shoulder blades for luck, before Tori and I hopped into the back of the buggy and we chugged away. The last thing we saw as Matt swung us round the corner was maybe – just maybe – Mum and Dad's free hands brushing together like they were thinking about joining up.

'I hope—' I began.

'Don't jinx it,' warned Tori, so I shut up.

Joe was a little pale, but smiling, at school the next day.

'Dad's collecting me,' he told us. 'We're going swimming. He's going to collect me every day this week.'

'If my parents did that I would *well* kill them,' said Cazza.

'Why?' said Tori.

Cazza looked astonished that Tori had even asked. 'They're *parents*.'

'I like our parents,' said Tori.

My sister had never quite grasped the rule about never saying nice stuff about your folks when on school property.

'Lucky you,' Cazza said sulkily.

'Dad says he told his boss that he wants to work at home once a week as well and his boss says he can,' Joe went on, beaming. 'So you guys can come back to mine maybe sometimes after school.'

This was pretty noteworthy. We never went round to do stuff at Joe's place. It looked like Mr Morton had finally started being a proper dad.

'Pavlov Valkyrie is going to do some filming at Wild World,' I said, keen to share our news as well.

Biro looked up from drawing his usual horses. 'With Mirza Khan again?'

'Just Ivana,' I explained.

'It's not *totally* fixed yet, Taya,' Tori reminded me. 'Mum needs to reintroduce Boris to his mum this week – you know that.'

Mr Valkyrie hadn't been very happy when Mum introduced this condition to filming Ivana, but he had accepted it.

'The handover will be fine,' I said confidently, flapping a hand at Tori. 'They'll be filming next week, you wait and see.'

I'd seen how well the Grandpa/Honey handover had worked – the little chimp was now happily scampering around with the other chimpanzees in the ape house and hardly gave us a glance through glass these days. I know Mum had said that reintroducing a bear cub was difficult, but I was an optimistic sort of person. With people like Mum and Dr Nik on standby, how hard could it truly be?

'Ivana might do *what*?' I asked in horror back

at home that evening.

'Eat Boris.' Mum finished giving the fluffy bear cub his evening feed and tickled him under the chin.

Tori looked a bit ill. 'Properly eat him or just take a bite?'

'Bears are very unpredictable,' Mum explained as she went over to the sink to put Boris's milk bottle in the dishwasher. 'Anything could happen. But we need to be prepared for the worst.'

'You can't let her eat him!' I said frantically. 'That's . . . *gross.*'

Mum shook her head. 'It's nature, Taya.'

'What's the best way of improving Boris's chances?' Tori asked.

'Dr Nik and I have been working on this all day,' Mum said. 'The cycling is critical, we think. We must make sure she has a good day on her bicycle and is in the best possible mood for receiving him.'

'Has the old bike from the film people arrived?' I asked, realizing at last what a total balancing act the filming and Boris's reintroduction was going to be.

Mum looked a bit tense. 'It's coming tomorrow morning. If she hates it . . .'

'Boris is more likely to get eaten, so Ivana will have to have her old bike back and the filming won't happen,' I said, working it out.

There was a depressed silence as we thought about waving goodbye to all those noughts. Matt and Mum had major plans for the money.

Boris flopped down in Rabbit's basket, practically squashing Rabbit flat as she was in there already. His leg was fine, and now he was really into sitting on us and stopping us from going places. I wondered if he'd picked up the trick from the time Ivana had sat on *him*.

'How's Dad?' said Tori, changing the subject. 'Did he come over today?'

We still hadn't worked out whether Mum and Dad had sorted stuff out on their walk to Matt's the night before. Dad had sloped off after the tea, muttering about seeing us soon but not exactly doing celebration handstands – at least not in our line of sight.

'He's well, Tori,' Mum said, 'and yes he did come over for a visit.'

Tori and I exchanged low-fives as unobtrusively as we could. Mum sat down at the table and reached for our hands.

'*Queridas*, we are so sorry you have seen us fighting so much,' she said. 'We have been very unfair to you.'

I felt breathless with hope. 'So is Dad coming back?'

'Not yet,' Mum said gently. 'But I hope it will be soon.'

In bed that night, Tori and I once again had too much to talk about.

'What's the delay with Mum and Dad, do you think?' I said, biting my thumb as I lay back in my bed.

'Dad probably hasn't dared to kiss her yet,' Tori said.

I groaned. 'Dad is so rubbish at that stuff. I mean, what's so hard about kissing your wife? Husbands do it all the time.'

'Mum can be a bit unpredictable,' Tori pointed out.

The word made me think of Ivana. 'She won't eat him,' I said indignantly. 'Not literally anyway.'

We both heard Boris's claws on the stairs outside our room. He nosed open the bedroom door and stared inside. A powerful waft of bear tickled our noses. I got out of bed and wandered over to see him and give his ears a rub. He groaned at me and shoved me so hard I fell down on my bottom.

'No, Boris,' I began, but he'd already sat on me. He was so heavy that I couldn't push him off by myself.

'Give us . . . a hand . . . Tor,' I panted. 'Push . . . Boris off, will you?'

'No way, Santa Fé,' said Tori. She propped herself up on one elbow so she could see and enjoy my small problem better. 'Let's call it payback for your little moment of diva fever at Harting Park.'

I groaned and lay back. My sister had always liked the idea that revenge was best served cold. Boris spread himself out a bit more comfortably, pressing even more of me into the floor.

'Partial payback, anyway,' Tori went on. 'I'll think of something else in a day or two, I expect.'

I knew defeat when I saw it.

'MUM!'

22

Completely Bamboozled

It was a relief to hurry down to the bus stop at the end of Thursday. Charlie-on-the-gate waved us into Wild World as he always did; a couple of people coming out looked at us, obviously wondering why two girls in Forrests school uniform weren't buying tickets.

The bear enclosure was quite near the entrance. Crowds of people were gathered around as usual: Ivana was big news these days. When we pushed to the front, we saw a brown bike with high handlebars and thin tyres lying near the bear house. It looked *ancient*, but probably wasn't. There was no sign of Ivana.

'Has she used it?' Tori asked a nearby lady.

The lady wrinkled her nose. 'Not since I've been

standing here,' she said. 'I'm not sure if I approve of a bear riding a bicycle anyway.'

Matt had printed out the story behind Ivana and her bicycle and it was pinned up on the fence for everyone to see. Maybe the lady was a bit shortsighted.

Tori and I pushed back through the crowd and went round to the bear house. Peeping through the little viewing window, we could see Ivana lying peacefully on her side with Anna and Sasha noshing away on her teats.

'She *looks* cheerful enough,' said Tori doubtfully. 'Don't you think?'

But it was impossible to tell.

Mum looked up from grooming Boris's tummy as we crashed through the front door five minutes later. Rabbit brought us a tea towel as a welcome-home present and dropped it at our feet.

'How was school, *queridas*?' Mum asked.

Why did parents always ask that incredibly boring question? School was school. Did they think we abseiled down the science block, or held our teachers to ransom, or rollerskated down the corridors wearing crazy hats? *Honestly*.

'Fine,' I said, kicking Mum's question and the tea

towel out of the way. 'Does Ivana like her new bike?'

'She has tried it, but only for a very short time,' Mum told us. Boris rolled on to his front and lay across Mum's feet like a massive furry draught excluder. 'We need her to ride it properly before we can know if it is a success. Dr Nik and I don't want to risk reintroducing Boris until we're certain Ivana is one hundred per cent happy.'

'But the filming's supposed to happen *next week*,' I said. Why was time so against us?

'If we rush it, Boris could end up eaten,' Tori said wisely.

'And if we don't do it in the next few days, we'll run out of time and Ivana won't accept Boris anyway!' I said. Have you heard of that expression, caught between a rock and a hard place?

'Mr Valkyrie knows the situation,' Mum sighed. 'We can check Ivana's progress again when the park closes.'

Tori and I spent a listless hour and a bit doing our homework and watching the clock. When the hands crept round to five-fifteen, Mum snapped leads on Boris and Rabbit and we all headed back out through the lamplit park to the bear enclosure.

The antique bike was still lying in the same spot, which wasn't very encouraging. Dr Nik and Matt were deep in conversation by the bear house. They both smiled as they saw us.

'She hasn't tried the bike since lunchtime,' Matt said, before we had a chance to ask. 'But she's being very calm with the cubs, which is a good sign. I'd just like to feel more confident that this new bike isn't going to cause problems before I—'

Ivana padded out of the bear house, blinking in the lamplight. She sniffed around the bike and picked it up. It took her a couple of attempts, but on the third go she was off and riding to the far side of the enclosure, her furry back tall and straight as her legs moved the pedals round, the park lights casting her bulky shadow in all kinds of strange directions.

'She looks more comfortable than on the other one,' Dr Nik said.

It was because of the seat position, I decided – it looked lower down, giving Ivana's upper body more room to hold the handlebars comfortably. Boris grunted with interest at the spectacle. He padded over to the fence on his lead and sniffed in his mother's direction.

We watched the big bear for ages. Round and round she went, like she was doing laps in some kind of Victorian bicycle Grand Prix. Judging from the relieved expressions on Mum, Matt and Dr Nik's faces, it was exactly what they'd been hoping to see.

At last Ivana stopped pedalling and shambled back into the bear house. We all took turns peeping through the viewing window into the den. As Rabbit and Boris sniffed noisily around my feet, I got a glimpse of Ivana tenderly licking Anna's head.

'Looking good,' said Tori.

Which, let me remind you, is my sister's version of 'WAHOO!'

'I think we can try the reintroduction on Saturday,' Mum said happily as we all came back outside again. 'We give Ivana plenty of cycling between now and then, get her some chest rub for her nose, put Boris in with his sisters, and see how we get on. Agreed?'

I followed Mum's reasoning – up to a point.

'Why does Ivana need chest rub?' I asked in mystification. 'Has she got a cold?'

'We'll rub Boris with some of his sisters' old bedding, but bears have an extraordinary sense of smell and Ivana may still sniff out the difference and turn on him,' Dr Nik explained. 'By putting chest rub on Ivana's nose we can guarantee that her sense of smell will be completely bamboozled.'

'No way,' said Tori, looking amazed.

I started giggling. I bet the inventors of chest rub –
that greasy stuff you rub on your chest to help you
breathe through a stuffy nose – hadn't planned on
having any large brown bears as customers for their
product.

I knelt down so I was on Boris's level, and he looked
at me with his little black eyes. We would miss him,
even though he was a nightmare when he sat on us and
his little climbing stunts had pulled the curtain pole
out of the kitchen wall.

'It's nearly time to rejoin your family, little guy,' I
said softly in his ear. 'I hope you won't need it, but –
good luck.'

On Saturday, Dad arrived bright and early at the house.

'Couldn't miss the big reunion, could I?' he
said, rubbing his hands in the damp-squibbish
morning mist.

'Here's hoping there's more than one of those today,'
Tori whispered to me as Mum fussed about making
Dad a cup of coffee exactly the way he liked it – water
just off the boil, not too much milk, two sweeteners.
The only difference from normal was the absence of
Dad's favourite mug. The little things were the weirdest
part of life after a house fire.

Rabbit wasn't very impressed at being left behind, but it was easier to keep her at home today. Boris shambled quietly along beside Mum on his lead, sniffing away at everything as we walked, until we met up with Matt and Dr Nik at the bear house. Dr Nik had a tranquillizer gun slung over his shoulder, loaded with just enough dopey stuff to knock Ivana out for a short time. In the enclosure, the big bear was already taking a spot of early-morning pedalling exercise.

We waited until she was finished. When Ivana eventually climbed off the bike and headed back towards the den, Dr Nik put his tranquillizer gun to a space in the fencing. There was a gentle pop. Ivana jumped briefly as the dart hit her in the leg and slid down on to her tummy like she was getting into position for a bit of tobogganing. Her eyes fluttered sleepily, then closed altogether.

'We've got about five minutes,' said the vet, putting down the tranquillizer gun and pulling on a pair of sterilized gloves. He took a pot of chest rub from his pocket. It looked just like the stuff in our medicine cupboard. In fact, it probably *was* the stuff from our medicine cupboard. 'I'll put this on Ivana's nose. You take Boris into the den, Anita.'

Matt unlocked the enclosure gate and Dr Nik

disappeared inside. Mum tugged the little cub along to the bear house and Boris followed her willingly. Tears blurred my eyes as they disappeared from view. What if . . .

'It'll be fine,' Dad said.

'How can you be sure, Dad?' Tori asked.

Dad glanced after Mum's disappearing back. 'Let's just call it a good feeling,' he said – and for a minute we wondered if he meant Mum or Boris.

We waited tensely with Dad. I pictured the scene: Mum reaching into the den for handfuls of the smelly straw bedding that had been deliberately left in the den for longer than usual – rubbing it all over Boris's soft brown fur to transfer the smell – opening the door into the den and passing Boris swiftly inside with one last tickle behind his ears. What would Anna and Sasha do? Hopefully they were too well fed to care too much about the intruder.

Dr Nik came out of the enclosure, stripping off his gloves. As Matt locked the gate again, Ivana began to shake her head groggily, as if wondering where on earth the weird eucalyptus smell was coming from. With a snort she got to her feet and looked around, checking that all was normal.

A wail that sounded suspiciously like Boris wafted

out into the enclosure towards her. Ivana responded at once, trotting at speed towards the bear house and squeezing inside. Silence fell.

Was that good?

We waited, and waited, and waited some more.

The tension started doing my head in.

'I'm going over to see how they're getting on,' I said after what felt like an entire decade of picturing Boris getting bitten and hurt by his unpredictable mother. 'Just a peep through the viewing window.'

'I wouldn't—' Dad began.

I was already jogging towards the bear house. Tori's footsteps weren't far behind.

'This could be awful,' Tori warned, catching up with me.

I wordlessly took my sister's hand as we ducked inside. Mum was crouched by the viewing window, as still as a stone. She glanced round and raised a finger warningly to her lips as Tori and I peered into the dimness of the den.

Ivana looked as if she'd fallen asleep, lying comfortably on her side in the straw. One, two . . . three little bears all sat in a peaceful row at her teats, feeding away like furry truckers in a roadside caff.

23

Total Wetsville

We left Boris and his family alone until Tuesday so they could get used to each other all over again. Rabbit was missing Boris terribly and moping around like a large yellow floor mop. While everything was a bit quieter and there was less fur to hoover up around the kitchen table, it was fair to say Rabbit wasn't the only one.

'Can't we just peep through the viewing window again—' Tori began on Monday evening.

'No,' said Mum.

I tried as well. 'Please, Mum. Pleeeeease . . .'

'We must give Boris every chance to bond with his mother and his sisters. The bear enclosure is closed until tomorrow from all prying eyes – ours as well as the public's. Now, I don't want to hear another word about it or I will go mad!'

Mum seemed strangely ratty for someone who'd just successfully reintroduced a young bear cub to his family. We hadn't heard anything from Dad since he'd left us with hugs, a manly handshake for Dr Nik and an awkward cheek-kiss for Mum on Saturday morning, and now it was Sunday afternoon. He really needed to move things along or Mum was likely to explode. Plus the weather – total wetsville – wasn't helping the general air of tension.

By Monday night, it felt like we'd had about a million bathtubs of water dumped on us since Saturday afternoon. Tori and I sat in our bedroom doing our homework – well, Tori was doing it anyway – and I painted my toenails an awesome purple and stared out of the window. A few soggy ostriches stood out in the middle of their field, raindrops falling off the ends of their beaks. We could hear the hippos roaring happily in their little lake by the tropical house. I hoped Boris was warm and cosy and full of Ivana's milk and love – and not forgetting about us too quickly.

'It would be weird, wouldn't it,' I said, 'if, like, you or I had been taken away from Mum—'

'Because she was trying to eat us?' Tori enquired.

I was determined to get to the end of my thought before I forgot the beginning. '—and fostered with someone else completely and then put back with Mum and each other again. Don't you think?'

'To be honest, Taya, I've never thought about it,' said Tori. 'What's the French word for "tomorrow"?'

'*Demain*.' I took pride in pronouncing it just right, and watched as Tori carefully wrote it down on Mr Jones's homework sheet. 'And talking about *demain*, I think Mr Valkyrie is sending some people over tomorrow to build Ivana's set ready for the filming on Wednesday.'

Tori put her pen down. 'They won't build the whole circus set around Ivana's enclosure in just one day. That's impossible. Are you sure the filming's on Wednesday?'

I was *fairly* sure that's what Mum had said, but now I thought about it, even the movie industry was going to have a bit of trouble building an exact replica of a Victorian circus tent in the pouring rain in just twenty-four hours. Weren't they?

'Yes,' I said firmly, deciding to ignore the whispering doubts in my head. 'Perhaps Mr Valkyrie has the weather on speed dial. "Hello, raincloud? I will make film today. No rain, OK?"'

* * *

If Mr Valkyrie was on speaking terms with the weather, then by Tuesday afternoon it was clear they'd had a major argument. We sloshed off the bus in sodden shoes and socks, trailing our bags through the puddles, our spirits as wet as the hems on our skirts and our drippy tendrils of hair. There was no way on this earth that anyone was going to be building film sets in this weather, even if everything was fine with Ivana and the cubs. If it kept up like this, there'd be no filming at all.

'What's the matter with you and your miserable faces?' Mum demanded as we surfed through the door on a tidal wave of rainwater. She was looking tired, her eyes dark and baggy and her hair scraped back with what looked suspiciously like a clothes peg. 'How was school?'

'Fine,' we both said automatically. Which was true if you ignored the bonfire of plastic school chairs that someone had attempted to light in the assembly hall. Theories had flown around the canteen at lunchtime until Cazza had spotted the Year Ten arsonist being marched off the premises for the second time that term.

'Have you seen the bears today, Mum?' I asked. 'Is everything OK?'

The irritable frown on Mum's face lifted. 'I took a little look this morning. Boris was curled up as cosy as can be with his sisters. Everything is as good as we could have hoped for.'

Suddenly my wet feet and cold damp collar didn't seem to matter. We all beamed stupidly at each other for a few seconds. Boris was safe and settled.

'But the filming's been postponed, right?' Tori checked. 'It's not happening tomorrow?'

Mum frowned again. 'Boris is settled and everything is fine. Why do you think the filming is not happening?'

'They haven't built the set,' I said patiently.

'Of course they have built the set,' said Mum.

Tori and I exchanged astonished looks.

'They built the whole thing today, in the rain?' Tori asked. 'They must have been up to their knees in water!'

Mum's look of confusion evaporated. 'Yes,' she said, smirking slightly like she knew something we didn't. 'Everything they need is in place. They will start filming tomorrow afternoon.'

I'd believe *that* when I saw it. I looked at my sister to exchange a 'Yeah, right!' kind of eye-roll and was surprised to see this sudden flash of understanding sweeping across her face like wind on a barley field.

Catching Tori's expression, Mum laughed.

'What's the secret?' I said. 'Is there something you're not telling me?'

'I just worked it out,' Tori answered, grinning. 'You should be able to work it out too, sis.'

I hated it when Tori did this – all Queen of Smug because her brain had crossed the finishing line before mine had even got its little grey cells in the starting blocks.

'What?' I demanded.

But Mum and Tori weren't telling.

It rained most of Wednesday too, so I made the most of Tori and Mum's most definite error of judgement and told our mates the filming would be off until further notice.

'It *is* still going to happen,' Tori insisted for the hundredth time as we came outside at the end of the day into what felt like the first flush of sunshine since for ever. 'Why can't you just believe me, Taya?'

I made a show of thinking. 'Um . . . possibly because . . . *it's totally and completely impossible?*'

'I'll bet you a full month's loan of my new *Doctor Who* boxed set that Taya's right,' Cazza commented, biting into an apple and spraying out the pips like machine-gun bullets on the playground tarmac. 'I mean, I know she's only got half a brain cell but you gotta look at the evidence.'

'Excuse me?' I demanded.

'Two months,' said Tori.

Cazza thought about this. 'And what do I get if Taya's right and you're wrong?' she checked.

'Taya will dance on a canteen table tomorrow afternoon,' said Tori. 'With a pair of knickers on her head.'

As Joe and Biro both burst out laughing, I boggled at my sister in horrified disbelief.

'I'll *what*?'

24

A Very Dead Knickers-on-the-Head-Wearing *Freak*

Tori – if you'll excuse the pun – weathered me hissing at her like a kettle of rattlesnakes for the whole of the ride home.

'Have you gone totally insane? Are you planning to ruin my life for ever and infinity and beyond? Why make a promise with *me* in it? Why not that *you'll* be the one doing the dancing? I mean, *what in wombat's name*? Is this part two of your revenge thing because you're still mad at me about the fight at Harting Park?'

'Yes,' said Tori happily.

'I'm related to a madwoman,' I moaned, clutching my head. 'A person with more nut content than a bird feeder.'

Tori got off the bus with a little skip of pleasure.

'As if dancing on a canteen table wasn't bad enough, you had to bring *knickers* into it!' I raged. As I jumped off the bus, I landed in a ginormous puddle practically up to my neck, which did nothing for my mood. 'Sweet sausage and mash! I swear, Tori, one of these days . . .'

Tori walked ahead of me past the signs that said *PARK CLOSED TODAY*, past Charlie-on-the-gate, as fresh and unruffled as a new tube of toothpaste. 'Cheer up, Taya,' she said over her shoulder. 'A pair of knickers on your head will suit you. You can put your hair in bunches and feed them through the leg holes.'

Ivana's bike was lying on its side near the bear house when we reached it. There was a new bit of extra-tall fencing at the back of the enclosure, while a quiet electricity generator, a group of darkened lights and a couple of lonely cameras draped in waterproof tarpaulins stood to one side. There was absolutely no sign of Mr Valkyrie, his crew or – most importantly – a big Victorian circus tent stuffed with extras in frilly costumes.

'I'm right and you're wrong,' I moaned, unable to enjoy my victory even the tiniest little bit. 'Which means Cazza just won her bet and I'm dead. Deader than a very dead knickers-on-the-head-wearing *freak*.'

'Quiet today, isn't it?' Tori said conversationally. 'That'll be because the park's closed for filming.'

I gestured in despair at the very un-Victorian-looking enclosure, the strange new fencing, the draped and silent lights and cameras. OK, so the sign on the gate had said the park was closed today. But what more evidence did my sister want that the filming just wasn't happening?

Mum and Mr Valkyrie suddenly crested the hill like a mirage, accompanied by a team of camera people, Dr Nik, Matt, several other Wild World zookeepers I recognized by sight – and Dad. The tarpaulins were hauled off the cameras and the generator was switched on, the lights illuminated the new fencing – a bright blue colour – at the back of the enclosure, and the scene was transformed from silent and still to a flurry of professional busyness in the wink of an eye.

'Hi, girls,' said Dad, coming over to give us beardy kisses.

'Where have you *been*?' Tori asked. 'Mum's been going completely crazy!'

Dad glanced over at Mum, who was carefully not looking in our direction and talking to Dr Nik. 'A job locating penguins in the north kept me away for a few days. Sorry I didn't call.'

A peculiar vision of Dad finding penguins waddling around Manchester city centre added an extra dreamlike quality to the muddle in my head.

'Glad you're back from school in time to see the filming anyway,' Dad went on. 'We've tried a few shots but Mr Valkyrie hasn't got what he's after yet. Ready to watch some magic?'

Tori slipped her arm through mine. 'Course we are,' she said cheerfully. 'Aren't we, Lady Gaga?'

'I don't understand,' I said in a small voice, looking down at Tori's arm and then back up at Dad and the mystifying scene before me. 'Where's the tent? Where are all the extras and all that stuff we had at Harting Park?'

'We don't need tent,' said Mr Valkyrie, looking round from a conversation he was having with a scared-looking cameraman. 'We shoot against blue screen and we add details after.'

'It's known as CGI,' Dad explained. He smiled in amusement. 'Were you expecting Harting Park all over again?'

I flushed a deep and very unflattering shade of roasted beetroot. How could I have been so dim? I'd watched those behind the scenes at the movies type documentaries hundreds of times. The actual set wasn't necessary any more. Ivana on her bicycle would be shot against the special screen and then they'd add the scenes they'd shot at Harting Park as a background. When Mr Valkyrie and his team of computer experts had finished with it, the whole thing would look completely seamless and believable.

'You're dead,' I said through gritted teeth as my sister howled with laughter and called me Lady Gaga a few more times.

'Let's just say we're quits, sis,' Tori choked.

The chatter hushed as Ivana put her long brown nose out of the bear house and sniffed around. Mr Valkyrie nodded and the cameras started rolling as she trotted over to her bicycle and pulled it upright for a couple of laps around her new, strangely blue enclosure. Round she went, once, twice, three times, before dropping the bike and trotting back into the den.

Through the waves of embarrassment still washing over me, I found enough brain space to think about how Boris was only a few metres away, safe and hidden in the darkness. It would be nice, I thought, if he poked his nose out to say hello. Bear cubs don't usually leave their dens until they're around ten weeks old, but

Boris's time away from his family had probably given him more confidence than his sisters where the big wide world was concerned.

'No, no, no!' shouted Mr Valkyrie, waving his hands around. 'Not enough! We need more!'

The camera people went into an earnest huddle as Mr Valkyrie put his face dramatically in his hands for a few moments before looking up again. 'Another take,' he pronounced. 'We wait for bear again.'

Dr Nik had drifted away from Mum and was now talking to Matt. Dad shuffled a bit closer to where Mum was standing, pretending to be looking at his watch.

Once again Ivana appeared at the mouth of the bear house. The cameras leaped into action as, this time, she brought a little bit of extra magic with her that made everyone gasp.

Boris peeped out at the brightly lit enclosure from his position on his mother's shaggy brown shoulders. He made an enquiring little groan and Ivana groaned back. I imagined the conversation with delight.

'*What's that, Mum?*'

'*A bicycle, son. It's a lot of fun. But don't ask me about the blue bit. It wasn't there yesterday.*'

Dr Nik started forward as Ivana rambled out into

the enclosure with Boris on her back like a hairy bright-eyed jockey. 'The cub may be in danger from the bicycle, Mr Valkyrie,' he said anxiously. 'We need to stop the filming and shut Boris back in the den.'

Mr Valkyrie nodded and raised his hand to stop the cameras. But it was too late. Ivana had already picked up the bicycle and climbed aboard – with Boris still on her back.

Ripples of electric excitement coursed through the air as Ivana pedalled around the enclosure, as stately as a queen on wheels, her passenger enjoying the free ride with his nose in the air and his tufty little ears blowing about in the wind. I had both hands pressed over my mouth, trying to stop the squeals of amazement from escaping. Beside me Tori was hopping from foot to foot, doing precisely the same thing.

Ivana and Boris made four circuits before Ivana brought the bicycle slowly to a halt. Somehow Boris stayed on her back as the mother bear dismounted and dropped back on to all-fours, suddenly in a hurry to return to the darkness of the den. As the two rumps, one large topped off by one small, disappeared from view, we had approximately five seconds of purest silence before Mr Valkyrie gave a yodel of triumph and punched the air. The cameramen all started shaking hands with everyone and anyone they could find – the zookeepers, Matt, Dr Nik. We all knew that something truly extraordinary had just been captured on film.

'Mum!' I shouted, whirling round ecstatically. 'Dad! Did you—'

The words died in my throat as I saw my parents kissing each other to death under the nearest lamp post.

'I'm not sure they were watching,' observed Tori.

25

Destined for Stardom

I stood on the red carpet at the front of the Empire Leicester Square, enjoying the moment. It was over six months since Boris had made his legendary appearance riding on Ivana's back, and I'd just seen it all over again. But what I'd seen this time had been pure and perfect circus from start to finish – even the bits that hadn't been set in the Big Top.

There had been all those Christmassy scenes at Harting Park – I remembered the snowdrift outside the front door a little *too* well – plus lots more stuff set in London and other bits of the countryside that were totally new to me. Goran the horseman had fallen in love with Rose de Lacey and made my heart hurt with the romance of it. There'd been Ellie in her pretty dresses; Lady Tempest full of magnificent anger and scorn – and more than a dollop of pure Joe-ness about her eyes. In the Big Top itself, Biro had ridden across the screen with his eyes alight, with Uncle Ardalan and the cousins and the gorgeous Kurdish horses that were so very different from Starlight and her friends. The air had rung with shouts and calls and applause, both on-screen and off. There'd been music too, in place at last, and the thump of hooves and feet on sawdust. And Ivana and Boris had ridden out across the ring to gasps of amazement and an explosion of applause, in the tent with all its bunting, its baskets of flowers and its cute little adverts for Victorian weirdery, for all the world as if they'd been there all along.

Tori came to stand beside me as the carpet filled up with chatting film people, all togged up in black tie and beautiful dresses. Mum and Dad were holding hands very tightly, deep in conversation with Mr Valkyrie while photographers blasted the air with flashes of light and shouts of 'Over here! Over here!' Joe looked very grown up in a dinner jacket that matched his dad's, looking on as Mrs Morton smiled and posed in her long red dress, with his dad's arm around his shoulders. Biro was laughing and joking with his family and Mirza Khan; Dr Nik was looking loved up with a blond-haired lady friend; and Matt's face was redder and more cheerful-looking than I'd ever seen it. Tori and I smiled and waved and giggled at the thought of all those photographers wondering who on earth we were, because we were neither famous nor in the film.

I couldn't quite resist it.

'Shame they cut your bit, Tor,' I said breezily. I fiddled with my long green dress, loving the way the light caught the wavy shiny lines of the threads in the skirt. 'I suppose it was Ellie's last scene and they didn't really need it. But you were probably disappointed.'

Tori looked surprised. 'They cut it? I didn't notice.'

'Seriously?' I said in disbelief. 'You mean, you weren't watching out for it?'

'I forgot,' Tori said absently. Her eyes suddenly brightened as she looked over my shoulder. 'Ooh! I really want to go and talk to that guy. He did the blue-screen effects with Ivana and Boris – and apparently he's working on the latest series of *Doctor Who*!'

Miss Geek UK rushed away, her silky blue trousers billowing around her legs. I felt a little deflated, to say the least. Then I saw Ellie and waved, my irritation with my totally unbelievable twin all but forgotten.

'Hey! Do you remember me? How are you? How was the Czech Republic?'

'Of course I remember you,' Ellie smiled. She looked amazing in a plum-coloured dress that trailed along the ground behind her. 'The Czech Republic was OK, I guess, but I missed my sister's wedding, which was kind of a bummer.'

I blinked. 'That's not good.'

'I know,' Ellie sighed. 'And I was supposed to be a bridesmaid.'

I couldn't imagine missing Tori's wedding for a film – especially if I'd been asked to be a bridesmaid. Maybe I wasn't really destined for stardom at all. Mind you, after the disaster of my one and only stab at a screen test, that was probably all for the best.

Mr Valkyrie loomed up, along with Mum and Dad. He kissed Ellie on both cheeks, then took my hand and kissed my fingers, making me squirm with embarrassment.

'Don't tell my actors,' he said, straightening up, 'but bears are star of my film. Tell me, did little bear ever do bicycle ride again?'

I shook my head. 'Ivana still does it most days round the inner safety enclosure they built for her. But Boris? No, never.'

Mr Valkyrie looked pleased to know he'd caught a once-off on his film. 'I have present for you, young lady,' he said then. 'To say thank you. You made bears happen.'

'It was Ivana and Boris who did all the work, Mr Valkyrie,' I pointed out.

Mum and Dad smiled, their arms round each other, as Mr Valkyrie clicked his fingers. A minion scurried over with a giant flat box tied up with a big red bow.

'Oooh!' I squealed in excitement. I'd never been given anything so big before! 'Can I open it right now?' That's the thing with me. No patience at all.

The ribbons came away with a single tug of my trembling fingers. Nestled there in clouds of white tissue paper was The Dress. The pink velvet dress with waterfall folds and lace sleeves. The dress which had caused all the problems. The dress that I'd ripped in my fight with Tori.

A vision of knickers and a canteen table drifted into my brain. I swallowed.

'Thank you,' I managed to say, and Mr Valkyrie beamed.

'You will wear it to many parties, I hope,' he said.

I crossed my fingers behind my back. 'Definitely,'

I lied. 'Thank you.'

Between you and me, that dress was going straight to the back of my wardrobe.

KOALA CRAZY

'Get a move on, 7H!' called Ms Hutson. 'It's one o'clock already and we haven't reached the marsupial enclosure yet. I feel as if we're hiking to Australia for real.'

We were doing a project on Australia, so a trip to the world-renowned marsupial enclosure at Wild World completely hit the spot. We were armed with the class camera and drawing pads and quiz sheets, and the plan was for us to do a massive wall display that would give the same effect as walking through the bush to the sound of a didgeridoo, only quieter.

The amazing thing about the Wild World marsupial enclosure is that they keep the animals – kangaroos, wallabies, quokkas, wombats and koalas – together in open pasture dotted about with bush-type trees like eucalyptus and tea tree and special Australian daisies and flowers so the animals can feel at home even when the weather is being English, like it most definitely was today. Hopping and trotting about, noses to the ground or in the trees, the marsupials were peacefully snacking their way through the afternoon. The wallabies were perfect miniature versions of the big kangaroos and the snoozy-looking quokkas were miniature versions of the wallabies, while the fat wombats swayed along with their furry bellies practically touching the ground and the koalas gripped on tightly to the eucalyptus trees overhead and stared at the world with shiny black eyes.

My classmates scattered to different corners of the enclosure to do their projects. Huddled in my coat, I sat myself down on a bench and started sketching my favourite kangaroo – a lovely toffee-coloured one I called Caramel. Kangaroos are quite easy. As long as you do them standing up with massive back legs and tiddly front ones everyone knows what you're trying to draw, unless they maybe think you're doing a wallaby.

'Nice rabbit, Taya,' commented Joe, who was scribbling the eucalyptus trees and the way their bark dangled down from the trunks and branches like silvery party-popper streamers.

'It's a *kangaroo*,' I said, stung.

'Oh, sorry,' Joe said cheerfully. He put his pencil down and tried to rub a bit of warmth back into his fingertips. 'You know, if you forget that we're freezing and squint a bit and peer through the fence like the mesh isn't there, it's like being in actual Australia, isn't it?'

I put my pencil down glumly and wondered if I could borrow the class camera. I was clearly not cut out for marsupial portraiture of the drawn variety. Glancing across the enclosure, I spotted the camera in Cash 'n' Carrie's grubby little hands. Needless to say, they were using it to take pictures of themselves instead of the animals, and squealing with laughter as they did it. Where was Ms Hutson? She was normally straight on to trouble like a homing pigeon on elastic.

As I looked around for our strangely absent teacher, my eye was caught by a flash of movement in Caramel's pouch.

'Hey,' I said, prodding Joe in excitement. 'Look at that!'

'It's a kangaroo,' Joe explained. He waved his hand at the rest of the enclosure. 'There's loads of them.'

'I saw her pouch move! There must be a joey in there!' How cool would a photo of a tiny kangaroo joey be? I wondered if it would be the same colour as its mum. I had to get that camera, RIGHT NOW.

Joe laid down his pencil and squinted. 'Where?'

'There!' I said again. I packed my drawing pad away and prepared to race over and snatch the camera from

Cash 'n' Carrie. I was pointing so hard, my arm felt like it was stretching like Mrs Incredible's. 'See? Again! Joe, you need glasses if you can't see that!'

It was the silence that I noticed first, followed by the sight of Tori rushing up to me at full speed. Behind her, I could see everyone standing about in uneasy clusters, drawing pads abandoned on the ground or the benches. Cash 'n' Carrie had put the class camera down and had their arms round each other.

'What's happened, Tor?' I asked, my hackles rising like a scared dog.

'Do you know where Cazza is?' Tori said, looking anxious. 'No one's seen her since Ms Hutson took her iPod. I thought she'd followed me to the viewing house where I was drawing some wombats but she didn't follow me at all. She's vanished and Ms Hutson's going *nuts*.'

I spotted Ms Hutson now, standing on the little pebbled road and talking urgently on a mobile phone and looking more frazzled than a piece of morning bacon.

'She's probably gone to the shop,' Joe offered.

Tori shook her head. 'Ms Hutson's called them. She's called the main office too. All the keepers are on alert but no one's seen her. What if she's been kidnapped or something awful like that?'

'No way,' I said. We all knew never to accept lifts from strangers, and frankly if someone ever tried to pull Cazza into a car they'd probably get beaten up and really, really wish they hadn't tried it in the first place. 'She'll still be in the park somewhere. You'll see.'

I wasn't feeling nearly as confident as I sounded. Cazza Turnbull made her own rules. Who knew what went on in her head half the time?

'You'll see,' I said again.

But it sounded hollow, even to me.

with Lucy Courtenay ...

Q) Where did you get your inspiration for the WILD books?

A) My inspiration for the WILD books started with an abiding interest in the Harry Potter film owls. Where did the director get them from? How do you train owls? Despite their reputation for wisdom, an owl's large and amazing eyes take up so much room in its skull that its brain is actually pretty weedy. I happily imagined classrooms full of owls, learning how to swoop into shot on cue and deliver parcels with perfect accuracy. And then I thought how much fun it would be to come up with a family who have an animals-on-film business. I would have them visiting film sets and video shoots, learning about different animals as they went along and having mad animal-related adventures that their schoolmates could only dream about. Bingo, WILD was born!

Q) Are you more like Tori or Taya?

A) I think I'm more like Tori than Taya. I like to know everything before I make decisions, I am overly serious sometimes, I can be quick and sarcastic, I generally make sensible decisions and I was good at school. However, there are plenty of Taya bits in me too. I am easily distracted, I'm naturally optimistic, I know more about popular culture and famous people than I should, I love fashion, I talk too much and I can be scatty . . .

Q) What's your favourite kind of animal?

A) My favourite kind of animal is probably something soft and fluffy, particularly if it's a baby. Cats are a big thing with me: tigers, snow leopards, my own rather fat and bad-tempered tabby Crumble. But I recently saw some real live elephants for the first time, and was completely amazed by them. And you can't really describe an elephant as soft and fluffy, can you? Uh-oh. Some Taya indecisiveness creeping in here. I think as long as it's not a wasp, I'm pretty happy.

Q) What were your favourite books as a child?

A) My favourite books? Willard Price's ADVENTURE series had me completely engrossed from the age of seven. I learned about spitting cobras and poisonous jellyfish, clever dolphins and mighty tigers, huge anacondas and blue-tongued polar bears and magnificent whales and . . . Mind you, I loved stories about magic and school too. Enid Blyton and The Hardy Boys adventures were favourites, as were Tintin and Asterix books. Oh wombats! How is a person supposed to choose? Tori would know the answer to this one straight away. So perhaps I'm more of a Taya after all!

WILD

ON THE WEB

If you're mad about Lucy Courtenay's WILD series then visit the Hodder Children's Books website. Here you'll find news and reviews, as well as exclusive competitions and sneak peeks at other books in the series.

www.hodderchildrens.co.uk/wild